THE KING WAS IN

HIS COUNTING HOUSE

THE KING WAS IN HIS COUNTING HOUSE

A Comedy of Common-Sense

by

BRANCH CABELL

ILLUSTRATED BY CHARLES CHILD

Wildside Press: 2003

Published by
Wildside Press, LLC
P.O. Box 301
Holicong, PA 18928-0301 USA
www.wildsidepress.com

Wildside Press Edition: MMIII

FOR

HAZEL RASCOE

Here is youth's journey, and that journey's end,
As he recalls it that had love to lend
Zest to his living, and held faith his friend
Eternally, in Branlon's dim dear wood,—
Lost love that revelled with large lustihood,
Lost faith that found and then unfound all good
Under the sway of Branlon's swaggering king's
Kindly ordaining of high happenings,—
Ere love with faith lay slain by Time, who brings
Relentlessly, against the half-poet's prime
And too-brief laughter and futile ripples of rhyme,
Silence and gray cold wits, to aid cold Time
Coldly to hale these weaklings one by one
Out of fair Branlon, through carved gates, whereon
Each carving speaks of faith and love fordone.

PREFACE

To set forth a fundamentally true Italian story, about authentic sixteenth-century happenings, in somewhat the manner peculiar to the Jacobean playwrights of England when they dealt with their own private melodramatic Italy; to employ their abridgements, their heightenings, their omissions, and their lurid, flashing, sardonic, trope-loving, declamatory and deep-colored locale *in general, in the same instant that I avoided their disturbing additions to history wheresoever they thought that history needed to be improved upon; to regard the costume of their period, as they did, without any feeling of its being fancy dress demanding description, and to dismiss scenery also with their tacit acceptance of its unimportance in human living; to involve my thoughts rather steadily with their two main concernments, which I take to have been death and rhetoric; but to proceed staidly in prose where they, alternately, had floundered or had flown by means of their hit-or-miss blank verse, and would cause me, in comparison, to seem on a walking tour about a country wherein pedestrians were the most rare of phenomena: such, in brief, was my notion when, in reverie, I first engaged myself with the time-dimmed prototypes of Ferdinand dei Vetori and his family circle, and first thought about removing them, from out of their native sixteenth-century Italy, into the Italy of Jacobean drama.*

It was a land in which these once flesh-and-blood Italian princelings had remained, to the best of my knowledge, undomesticated. So far as I knew—or know to-day—no one of the Jacobean dramatists, who retold so many crime-crammed Italian stories, had used any considerable part of the tale told hereinafter.

Nor would I present this story under the vainglorious pretension of having invented it. Instead does honesty compel me here to admit that in the main my story is authentic, even though it be an historic chronicle so compressed and so abridged as to rehearse (just as did all the Jacobeans) within an indeterminable brief while the happenings of a number of years. For the fact that more or less everything which I relate did actually happen, in more or less the way I record, there is warrant always, either in the page of history or the bypath of legend. I concede, however, that in our imperfect world of flesh and blood, these matters could not very well happen with the agility which graces every sequence of events in that callous and eloquent and homicidal Italy which the Jacobeans for the most part imagined, and which they made fertile with melodrama.

After this much of comment as to the special origin and the special setting of my narrative, one may yet further remark that its theme is not at all special. My theme hereinafter, under whatsoever trappings of the ironic, remains, at every instant, that growth of altruism and of social responsibility which makes civilized every human life, should that life be prolonged sufficingly. Until some-and-twenty we are all of Cesario's kidney more or less, we are all egoists; and our young vanity prospers then; we blossom very wantonly, like a plot of narcissi, in that short springtime. But thenceforward, and forever after the death of boyhood, our innate self-centredness must flounder about in a losing battle, from which it may hope at best to withdraw with lessened forces. In brief, time puts upon us in thought, whether we will it or not, a marked respect for altruism; and compels us, in action also, to honor the tenets of altruism, or else be destroyed. I may not say that we come, quite, to love our fellow creatures; but, as we go on living, we do acquire a thither-to unfamiliar habit of allowing for their needs.

—Which sounds, I admit, trite. In point of fact, it is indescribably trite, because it happens, a little by a little, to every human being who is not fated to die either in youth or in prison; and it is the supreme shape-giver in the development of human character. I am not praising, any more than I reprehend, this time-forced altruism. I record merely, in this place, its existence—and its world-wide existence as perhaps the most dynamic of all strong forces in human life and in human civilization,— because in the pages which follow I have depicted the unchecked, if beneficent, tyranny of this altruism, in continuous action.

Through this tyranny (to which he surrenders without rhetoric) Ferdinand dei Vetori finds in his Melphé "an exorbitant mistress" just as my first chapter forecasts; and, after his own fashion, he serves that mistress with an unmagnanimous and prosaic loyalty. But Lorenzo, in his lax genial efforts to evade this tyranny, is destroyed,—as indeed (excepting only chance-murdered Gratiano) is destroyed everyone else who perishes in this book, inasmuch as each one of them meets ruin through a pursuit of some private interest which is at odds with implacable altruism. And lastly, by this same stringent great tyranny, Cesario becomes transformed, howsoever unwillingly, and despite his small peevish struggles, very much as, in the long run, this tyranny transforms most of us.

In brief, in the words of my final chapter, "Cesario becomes Ferdinand"; and after his allotted jaunt into Branlon he accepts more or less quietly his allotted place in the social organism of flesh-and-blood Melphé: that is my story. It is the normal story of all mankind.

St. Augustine, Florida
1935–1938

CONTENTS

PEOPLE OF THE STORY

THE POPE.

THE EMPEROR.

PAOLO D'ORSINI, Tyrant of Bracciano.

FERDINAND, Duke of Melphé.

CARNESCHI, the Duke's Prime-Minister.

LORENZO

GRATIANO

SEBASTIAN

CESARIO
} Sons to the Duchess of Melphé.

LYSANDER, a Greek Lord.

SIEUR DE LA FORÊT, a vagabond Scholar.

PESCARO, a Lord of Pania.

GLASIGNAC, a Lord of Bracciano.

MALANDRINO, Captain of the Duke's body-guard.

SACROBOSCO, an Assassin.

GRIMOARD, another Assassin.

GUIDOBALDO, a Poisoner.

ADORNI, a Tailor.

[xv]

PEOPLE OF THE STORY

Two Priests of St. Dominic.

Four Druids of Rorn.

Several Cardinals, Gentlemen of Poictesme and Melphé, Executioners, Spies, Judges, Gaolers, Tormentors, a Clerk, a Barber, Attendants, &c.

CATERINA DI SERLI, now Duchess of Melphé.

BEATRICE, her Daughter.

ISABELLA, the Duchess' second Daughter.

GIOVANNA D'ESTE, Wife to Lorenzo.

HYPOLITA, Daughter to Lysander.

HERMIA, his other Daughter.

Ladies of the Duke's court, Nuns of the Penitent Magdalene, Waiting Women, &c.

SCENE—The ITALY of Jacobean drama.

PART ONE: THE FAITH OF CARNESCHI

I

The time was evening, and the scene an upper room in the Governor's Palace at San Marco. That same afternoon the four sons of the newly made Duke of Melphé—those boys who, at all events, were the sons of Duke Ferdinand's wife—had aided to bury Duke Sigismund, the late tyrant over Melphé. It was he whom they now discussed.

"This Sigismund has gone to his final rewards; and charity commands us to speak of the dead with all deference," declared Gratiano dei Vetori, who was the second born of these brothers.

"Nevertheless," replied Lorenzo dei Vetori—to whom, as the dead man's bastard, the subject appeared thorny—"he was an indifferent ruler. He was distinguished, if at all, by his indistinction."

—Whereupon Cesario dei Vetori, the youngest of the four boys, looked up from the papers which at this instant he was assorting into nine piles upon a crimson-covered table. Cesario said:

[3]

"I admit only that he lived in hourly bondage to lust and terror. He was an unhappy man."

Then Sebastian dei Vetori, the third brother, mentioned loudly a natural function.

"He was an unhappy man! I agree with you, Master Scholar Cesario. That is the epitaph of all princes, by and large. Yet a reigning prince has his consolations."

"Very truly a prince finds his consolations," Cesario granted, "in all shades and in all shapings of sweet flesh. But not infrequently these consolations have husbands. And now and then these husbands have daggers.—Whence, upon a sudden, has our father become Duke of Melphé. As by-and-by you, Lorenzo, will also have become Duke of Melphé."

At that, Lorenzo was horrified.

"I pray Heaven, Brother Cesario, that any such event may be extremely remote."

"The sentiment reflects more credit upon your tact than your truthfulness," Cesario returned, smilingly,—"for a vast number of reasons."

"Indeed," says Lorenzo, coloring up, "but those reasons are as many as are the wild oats upon our family tree."

[4]

"Poot!" said Sebastian. "All Melphé knows that Sigismund was the father of Lorenzo. It is natural enough that Lorenzo should succeed him."

"This is ugly talk, this is not wholesome talk," cried out Gratiano.

"It is frank talk, such as suits my begetting, you smug son of nobody knows whom," said Sebastian. "Now, I was put into our mother's belly by an emperor; and I do not care who tells it."

"Be silent! and let us speak of more decent matters, you gross-mouthed idiot!" replied Gratiano.

Sebastian fingered his dagger.

"I do not practise silence, not I. Yet it is a priestly virtue, you sprouting abbot. Shall I instruct you in it?"

"To the contrary," said Cesario, "do you two cease your eternal squabbling."

"This patron of choir boys began it," said Sebastian, sullenly.

"I have good Scriptural warrant," said Gratiano, bristling, "when I answer a fool according to his folly."

"Miaow! Bow-wow!" says Cesario. "You two are like a cat and a dog, precisely. Be silent, both of you. Let us agree amicably, as befits four law-

[5]

abiding young princes of the blood, to accept that father whom the law, if not nature, has accorded the four of us. Such is the best policy, I submit, now that our father—our legal father, at all events, gentlemen,—has become Duke of Melphé."

He went then toward the open window, looking out upon the plaza.

"—Yet this Melphé," Cesario philosophized, "is a starved province, a lawless province. It has destroyed all them who attempted to master it. Of the dukes of Melphé, two have been killed in insurrections, three were assassinated. The first Ferdinand died in exile; Francesco, in a dungeon: and if Cosimo expired in his own bed, without so much undignified haste, yet it was through the aid of poison. Yes, gentlemen; the Duke of Melphé is a personage whom no sane person would envy. And just as we four, through the patient wiles of Carneschi, have become princes of the blood, overnight, as it were, just so our good mother's husband, who yesterday was not anybody in particular, has become the ninth Duke of Melphé. The results may be curious; I scent trouble: for this new Duke Ferdinand, I believe, will approach his new duties gravely."

"He will serve war-ravished Melphé," Gratiano amended, "not laxly, as did dead Sigismund, but to the utmost of his God-given ability."

Cesario answered: "Just so. It is that which I fear. I fear also that he may find starved Melphé an exorbitant mistress."

"The youngster becomes lewd," remarked Lorenzo. "His mind appears to be running always upon the theme of mistresses since he first saw that Greek girl Hypolita. He embarrasses me."

"But you three have not seen her," replied Cesario, conclusively. "And I shall take good care that you do not ever see her until she is safely my wife. Otherwise, there would be an end to our fraternal affection, because you three could not choose but worship her as whole-heartedly as I do."

Gratiano said: "Yes, my brother; but is it permitted you to make her your wife? Now that we are princes, our noble father must weigh most carefully whom we may or may not marry. It is an affair of state."

Cesario dissented.

"For Lorenzo and for Sebastian, that is true. You, Gratiano, I suspect, he will not permit to marry anybody. You are meant for the Church. In its holy confines, as a bishop, or it may be even as a cardinal, you will have to content yourself with a seraglio of mistresses—"

"No," said Gratiano, indignantly.

"—Of boys, then," Cesario assented, with a comprehending smile. "But it does not at all matter whom a fourth son may marry. A fourth son is not a personage. So a fourth son may ask hopefully for our noble father's consent—as indeed, I mean to do this very evening."

"Hoh, and the meek Duke," cried Sebastian, "will direct you to take your orders, in this as in every other matter, from his Huguenot master. Come now, but you know as well as we all know that it is Carneschi who rules over Melphé now that our noble father—so to style handsomely this kind, blind, philanthropic, wife-lending mackerel —has been dubbed Duke."

"You do not understand the true character of our mother's husband, my dear Sebastian," returned Cesario, gravely.

"Aha, Master Secretary! whereas you, I suppose, have this gray dirt at your fingers' ends!"

"It has been my privilege," Cesario admitted, "to assist Duke Ferdinand in sorting out the papers which were left by the late Duke Sigismund. It has been, I can assure you, a privilege which broadened my views as to the entire family of the Vetori. And that reminds me that, upon the stroke of eight, the new Duke wished me to bring him these two special packets."

"Come now, Brother Cesario, but the all-great Carneschi is with him."

"Yes; and indeed I rather fancy," replied Cesario, "that some such coincidence was intended. So I shall not ask for my Hypolita until after Carneschi's affairs have been disposed of. And that may not take very long, gentlemen," he remarked, portentously, as Cesario left the room.

"The boy knows something of importance," was Gratiano's comment.

"It is Cesario's unfailing failing," Lorenzo amended, with the unrelenting accuracy of close kinship, "to believe that he knows everything of importance."

II

A reflective person could not but meditate—as did Cesario, during the while that he walked from the company of his brothers toward the Duke's private closet—upon the state of affairs which the papers Cesario now carried were about to alter. Inasmuch, however, as these affairs involved the entire dukedom of Melphé, they are best rendered in the dignified phrasing of history, as concerns the busy month then ending.

The battle which decided the fate of Melphé (records the Abbot of Tarba) was fought upon the last day of April, in the plains north-west of Voldevurlo; and Carneschi there gained a complete victory which delivered into his hands all the opponents of his pawn and nominal master, Duke Ferdinand. The prisoners taken upon this occasion were very numerous: and of these some fifty-odd were Ferdinand's near relatives; whom the policy of Carneschi now condemned to a prompt loss of that blood which they were so unfortunate as to share with a prince whose legal rights to succession appeared more dubious than was the need to enforce them.

In brief, the inexperience of the new Duke was guided by the inexorability of his mentor into channels of a most repellent nature; and death labored daily to repair the deficiencies of Duke Ferdinand's

birth. He whom chance had brought forth in ob-
scurity, as a disregarded cadet of the younger
branch of the Vetori, was thus raised, through repeated homicides, to the desired status of being the
realm's lawful heir; and Ferdinand became beyond
cavil the legitimate head of his once vast family
connection, now that a parody of justice had curtailed rigorously the hosts of his living relatives.

Carneschi struck, again and again, with a continuing severity. The cells of the Forgello were
crowded with the kinsmen of Duke Ferdinand; and
when the Forgello could hold no more, then yet
other foredoomed scions of the Vetori glutted the
still darker dungeons of the Bartezza. The bed-
ridden uncle and both the surviving aunts of
Ferdinand alone, out of deference to their advanced
age, were respectfully garroted in a becoming and
dignified seclusion. Such indulgence, however, did
not prove habitual; for seventeen of his cousins,
irrespective of their age, their sex, their innocence,
or the perturbed pleasure of the public at large,
were executed in the thronged plaza of San Marco,
with a more ample leisure, day after day, while the
gaily painted salons of the Forgello rang with the
lamentations of the new Duke's ten nephews and

his three nieces under the sanguinary supervision of skilled tormentors. Of the once powerful Vetori, not one escaped a formal charge of high treason and sedition. Each was in turn convicted, under a cloak of impartial if necessarily hurried justice, after having been tortured by masked Ethiopians; and each was forthwith beheaded with the solemn respect due to a member of the reigning family.

Carneschi in this way, after a fortnight of arduous labors, removed all possible claimants to the position intended for his protégé; and then celebrated with exceeding splendors the funeral of the late Duke Sigismund, whose body had been left to decay, in the little chapel of Our Lady of the Milk, during the while that his relatives fought for his duchy. So was it that a remote cousin of Duke Sigismund succeeded to the last prince of the elder branch of the Vetori. No kinsman was left alive anywhere to dispute this Ferdinand's claim to be called Duke of Melphé; and over Ferdinand ruled Carneschi.

Of the new Duke, it is a singular reflection, no more was expected at this time than in reason might bud from the exiguity of his repute. He had been recognised thitherto but as the complaisant

Pandarus of a superb wife, whose charms had so far delighted his predecessor in Melphé and the nobility of seven kingdoms as to leave doubtful the paternity of all her children excepting only the first born, who was known to have been begotten by Duke Sigismund. As the hired husband of the Duke's put-by mistress, Ferdinand thereafter had thrived quietly upon the limited pension and the unconcealed contempt of his predecessor. He did not often accompany his wife to court except upon quarter-day; and his pre-eminent virtues had thus stayed virtually unknown until Carneschi took charge of his fortunes.

It may be recalled that Carneschi (in the more tranquil season of his early manhood, which preceded the repugnant spectacle of a Papal Protonotary's open conversion to the Lutheran error of justification by faith) had been employed as the tutor of Ferdinand dei Vetori, throughout the period of the latter's boyhood. During the prolonged and stormy career of Carneschi, this distinguished if misguided Huguenot had at no time dissevered communications with his former pupil. In the confusion attendant upon the death of Sigismund without any legitimate offspring, Carneschi had made adroit use of the circumstance that the murdered Duke had left a comely and amiable son, now approaching manhood, in the person of Count Lorenzo, whom the dictates of courtesy (in contravention to public knowledge) described as the oldest child of Ferdinand dei Vetori. Lorenzo therefore, in the course of nature, might quietly succeed his true father, should the claim of Ferdinand be allowed; and an elementary justice would thus be conceded without any violation of the proprieties.

The argument was specious, but three regiments backed it; and so, in due season, it prevailed. In this fashion (concludes the Abbot of Tarba) was the marital broad-mindedness of Ferdinand dei Vetori made his first stepping-stone toward that glory which now enshrines his name; and which keeps his memory immortal, in the proud annals of Melphé.

III

Thus far speaks the Abbot of Tarba; and inasmuch as his concern was with public matters alone, he then passes on to speak of the war against Ferrata and Pania. The Abbot, for this reason, does not record how Cesario, still bearing his two packets of papers, came into the Duke's private closet; and upon entering the small lamp-lit apartment, which was hung with bright gilded leather hangings and emblazoned everywhere with gay coats of arms, was waved aside by Duke Ferdinand absent-mindedly.

"Do you wait, though," says the Duke; and resumed his unfinished talk, with Carneschi, saying,—

"So this affair is quite settled, you believe?"

"It is well settled," Carneschi agreed, putting up the Pope's letter, "now that Ser Gratiano is named Cardinal of San Marco. The biretta has been tendered without over-much graciousness, to be sure, on account of some slight deficiencies in the friendship felt for me by the present Bishop of Rome. It is a sort of obsession with this former Grand Inquisitor"—Carneschi added, with a good-natured gesture of contempt. "Yes, highness; that old fanatic would torment and burn me also—even me, who am here duly certified to be his beloved son in Christ—with a vast deal of pious enjoyment. But his lunacies do not matter. We have got from him what we wanted far more than we wanted his

[15]

politeness. We have got the appointment which was needed for your second son."

"One must allow for the awkward position of the Holy Father of all Christendom," remarked Ferdinand. As a sound Catholic, the Duke preferred to talk about the Pope with proper respect. Then Ferdinand continued:

"His Holiness could not well relish having to deal with you in the affair, inasmuch as you quite openly seduced his mistress when he was merely the Bishop of Nepi. He resented any such sacrilege, of course, because she was a nun vowed to eternal chastity. Moreover, it appears a quaint notion, dear friend, that you, who are a confessed Protestant, should have the chief say in the making of a cardinal."

"It is in your service, highness, as well as for the good of all persons concerned. Ser Gratiano is a remarkably talented young man."

"He is perhaps the best of the litter," the Duke agreed, without much enthusiasm.

"I deplore the expression, sir: and I do not, of course, dare to allot pre-eminence to any special one of the four noble sons who adorn your family.

I say only that in what you Romanists misguidedly term holy orders, Ser Gratiano will climb far."

"Even to that topmost bough, I hope," says the Duke, "of which the fine fruit is a triple tiara. The Cardinal of San Sixtus, I suppose, will be the next pope after Pius. But old Hugo Buoncompagno becomes gratifyingly infirm; he will not live forever. By the time he enters into eternal bliss—through your loving aid, perhaps, if he needs it,—why, then you will have so managed affairs, I do not doubt, Carneschi, that Gratiano shall succeed him."

"That, highness, is for all practical purposes arranged. In the consistory, five cardinals will vote for us through motives of conscience; and we have purchased nine others."

Ferdinand leaned back, at that, and he regarded his prime-minister appreciatively, with frank admiration.

"Truly, you have a fine faculty for arranging matters, Carneschi; and a particularly sure hand for contriving this or the other departure out of living pat to your purpose. One cannot but envy you this most useful gift, through which you bid fair, at your present rate of progress, with lean

THE KING WAS IN HIS COUNTING HOUSE

Death as your ever-busy lieutenant, to control not Melphé but Christendom."

Carneschi shrugged.

"All Christendom knows, highness, that I control nothing except as your factor."

The Duke replied: "I am a rustic and slow-witted person. That is well understood, even by me. Yet my credulity has limits. You control me in everything: that also is understood, Carneschi, even by me."

"Highness," cried Carneschi, with a large exhibition of horror, which was perhaps more courteous than convincing, "highness, but your suggestion troubles me!"

"Oh, I do not complain. You have managed my worldly affairs far better than ever I could have managed them. You have made of me, who was yesterday but a quiet-living, impoverished country gentleman, the ninth Duke of Melphé. You have done this through what indirections, what bribes, what plottings, what knife-thrusts in dark alleyways, what lies, what jealous husbands, what sugared poisons—over and above your late massacre of my kinsmen,—I do not inquire. I am served zealously. Zeal contents me."

Under this sincere and well-considered praising, Carneschi displayed a becoming degree of modesty.

"Ah, but in time," says he, "in due time, highness, I shall make of you a reigning prince second to nobody."

"Yes," Ferdinand replied, gravely, "it is you who, in due time, will make me, not merely a duke, but a reigning monarch, the good brother of all other kings and sultans and emperors. I am wholly sure of that, Carneschi. The thought pleases me. And it seems a pity that my late cousin Sigismund was not so well served."

"A libertine! a mere loose chamberer!" says the prime-minister. "It passes belief that his lecheries were endured for so long; and no service could have protected him forever against the outraged husbands, the aggrieved fathers, and the over-worked bawds of Melphé."

"Yet he maintained his police, his informers, and his hired spies, no less than he did his panders."

"Mere prudence, highness, demanded that of him."

"Yes, Carneschi; for a prince needs to be both prudent and ruthless."

[19]

Now the Duke signed to Cesario; and the boy delivered to him two packets of letters.

Duke Ferdinand continued: "So his kinsmen were well observed, I discover. He had kept the reports which his spies rendered him as to his kinsmen. I have found these reports not undiverting. It appears that my deceased cousins, Luigi and Andrea and Francesco, as his next heirs, were permitted to conduct no earthly business—not in bed, not even in the dim quietude of the privy—without being spied upon faithfully."

"Doubtless," said Carneschi.

He now stroked his white beard with an air of reflective amusement. Not many persons knew more than did Carneschi about such matters.

"In particular," the Duke said, "have I been entertained by these special letters which relate to me. Your reports were most excellently expressed. You have an amusing and trenchant style, in addition to your other gifts."

Briefly Carneschi remained silent, still stroking his patriarchal beard. He spoke then, with benignant candor.

"I had thought it my duty, highness, to conceal from you the fact that now and then, during many years, I have been ordered by Duke Sigismund to report to him, in secret, upon your conduct and activities. It would have introduced into our life-long friendship an element of awkwardness, during the perplexed while that we waited for his iniquities to transfer him from his merely earthly honors to the superior delights of heaven. You would not have been candid, you would not even have been wholly at ease with me, highness, if you had known that a half sentence, in my enforced correspond-ence with Sigismund, might at any instant remove your head from your shoulders. And I valued your confidence, I was proud of it. I wished to retain your confidence."

The Duke said: "At heart I am a romantic. You should remember that, my tutor."

"I do remember that, Ferdinand," replied Car-neschi, in a strangely fond voice. "That has been your constant danger."

The Duke nodded in confirmation.

"I continue," he said, sadly, "to suspect human nature of being admirable. The years have not ever cured me, quite, of that quaint delusion. It is a large pity. As a result of this delusion, I have been troubled to discover that my assured friend, my trusted adviser, the young man whom during my boyhood I adored so whole-heartedly, was all the while a spy set upon me."

"So, highness, is your guardian angel in heaven. I may say boldly that upon earth I have reduplicated his rôle."

"Nor," says the Duke, reflectively glancing over the papers in his hand, "nor do I altogether agree with your description of the brutality of my nature, the profound baseness of my morals, and the incurable weakness of my intelligence."

"Indeed, sir, but in the reports which you are now holding, my loyalty has endowed you with every known form of extreme vice and stupidity. That, as I need hardly point out, was for your protection. Your cousin Sigismund was in this way persuaded he had no reason to fear you. I do not like to boast. Yet all the while that we were planning to remove him, it was my incessant calumny which, year after year, has convinced him that you were a dissolute imbecile rather than a budding rival."

There is no resisting sound logic; nor did Duke Ferdinand attempt the impossible. Instead, he admitted, with frankness:

"Truly, Carneschi, you are right. You were be-
traying both him and me; and you were being paid,
meanwhile, by both of us. If our plot succeeded,
you were sure of being well paid by me: if at any
time it appeared endangered, you had but to reveal
it to Sigismund; and then too you would be well
paid. Your policy had no flaw; and, believe me, I
do not criticize it except with entire admiration.
In this world one must live. Moreover, all these
matters appear trifles beside the fact that, as I now
learn, at the very beginning, when you were first
made my tutor, Carneschi, you poisoned Maria dei
Pazzi at my kinsman's orders."

The prime-minister nodded, assentingly, and
with some sadness.

"I regretted the necessity, highness. But you
loved the girl. There was no separating you from
her as long as she lived."

"So you murdered her, my friend, in order that
I might be forced, in my despair and my entire
misery— But what do I say? I mean that you arranged this matter also. You arranged for her
ascent into Paradise, in order that I might be rid
of all foolish entanglements and made free to marry
my present Duchess."

[23]

The Duke spoke without any special sign of any especial emotion. Yet he trenched upon awkward grounds, because, as has been recorded, everybody in Melphé knew that Ferdinand had been partly bullied, and in part paid, to marry the discarded mistress of his now deceased cousin, Sigismund, at a time when it was imperative a discreet husband be provided for her before the birth of Lorenzo, whom she was then carrying.

Carneschi, therefore, as befitted a rational person, answered with an air of not altogether concealed reproof,—

"That marriage, highness, was the beginning of your prosperity."

And the Duke replied, humbly enough: "Why, but of course! Had Maria lived, I would, in my absurd young folly, have married her. I would have remained an untroubled rural squire at Arvieto, a mere nobody, with Maria at my side always, as we passed hand in hand through life. She had very tender hands. I remember the soft, clinging, kindling touch of her hands, even after all these years. The girl loved me. But by murdering her you induced me to marry more sensibly, with a more noble cash profit. Yes, you have guided my fortunes unfailingly. It has moved me, Carneschi, to observe, in these old letters and in these quite recent letters, so many repeated proofs of the fine tirelessness with which you have removed honor and happiness from out of my life in order to make me Duke of Melphé."

"It has been my privilege to serve you somewhat, highness, and even in my humble degree to act as your benefactor," Carneschi admitted.

"Yes," says the Duke; "and I must endeavor to be worthy of your devotion. Do not doubt, dear friend, that so far as goes my ability, I shall repay you. Meanwhile, now that Cesario wishes to talk with me in private about his affairs, it may be that you would yourself prefer to destroy these papers. In unfriendly hands, you conceive, they would render possible your being hanged for murder; and in any case, they convict you of more treachery, and of more crimes, and of a larger number of lewd abominations, than any statesman would care to have attested by the ugly evidence of his own handwriting."

With that, the Duke handed to his prime-minister, somewhat slowly, Carneschi's account of how he had killed Maria dei Pazzi; and then, with a more lively gesture, the Duke tossed toward him the fat packet of obscene reports as to Ferdinand's private life which Carneschi had been making to dead Sigismund, off and on, throughout many years.

So was the affair concluded, to the perplexed disappointment of Cesario, who had stood waiting all this while; and Carneschi—after thanking Duke Ferdinand for his generosity, in terms of complete approval—withdrew from the apartment, taking with him the records of his double treachery.

IV

"Now then, Cesario," says the Duke, "what is it you want of me?"

Cesario answered that with a most happy combining of frankness, of true eloquence, and of four splendid similes; and from out of this display of flushed and brilliant imagery, Duke Ferdinand drew the correct drab inference. Cesario wanted to marry.

"Yet marriage," says the Duke, "marriage, in addition to being a holy sacrament, is likewise an affair of some importance. To unlegalized fornication, within reasonable limits, and with polite safe-guards, nobody can well object in the proper up-bringing of noble persons. As to that point, how-ever, you had perhaps best consult your mother."

"Sir," said Cesario, in some discomfort, "even though you have not the foibles proper to a hus-band, can you not respect the tender and pious emotions of a son?"

The Duke regarded the embarrassed boy, con-siderately, with very bright and keen and old-looking eyes, which twinkled; but sedate Ferdinand did not pursue the immediate subject. Instead, he asked,—

"Yet why need you marry the girl?"

It was a question to which Cesario replied by describing his own dear Hypolita, that goddess without any parallel, in the astounding phrases habitual to young poets. And the Duke listened to Cesario as if in meditation, even with a sort of quiet, grim affability.

"In my youth also," he stated, "earth harbored such paragons."

—Whereupon, from the purely descriptive, Cesario desisted. He passed on to the logical; and became persuasive.

There nowadays was not in Duke Ferdinand's nature any ill-advised tenderness toward romance, as Cesario well knew: for a reigning prince, it was wholly proper that the Duke should preserve, in this as in every other matter, his admired and most princely self-control. Such was the lad's frank exordium. Yet Ferdinand also had once been the victim of love's darts, even of love's delusions, it might be, as Cesario likewise pointed out. One lover should sympathize with another lover, if but *ex officio,* as a person with whom he had all in common,—provided of course that they did not have quite so much in common as to adore the same lady.

It was therefore in the revered name of Madonna Maria dei Pazzi that Cesario made his appeal, in the name of that unflawed paragon, so foully murdered, herself love's martyr, Cupid's most lovely and tender-handed saint. Cesario had first heard the name of Maria dei Pazzi some ten minutes ago, as he freely admitted: yet so great was his confidence in Duke Ferdinand's judgment that Cesario knew the object of young Ferdinand's affection could have been lacking in no kind of excellence. Well, and Hypolita was but by a very little inferior to Maria dei

Pazzi; the emotion with which Cesario regarded Hypolita was the same emotion which young Ferdinand had once felt for Maria dei Pazzi. That, apart from two metaphors and a free rendering from Lucretius as to the power of love, was Cesario's argument.

Moreover, as Cesario added in a more frankly practical vein, he had three elder brothers. The marriage of a fourth son did not come under the head of affairs of state, it was virtually negligible.

"That fact is perhaps your best advocate," Duke Ferdinand conceded—"so far as it goes."

"Indeed, sir, but precisely as you say, it is a wholly unanswerable argument," Cesario agreed, with enthusiasm.

"You must not put words into my mouth, Cesario. Even though I lack your hot flux of rhetoric, I can yet speak for myself at need. Well, and I was about to say that my good Gratiano is now, as you have heard, a cardinal. I design for him by-and-by the Papacy. Yes, he shall be the third pope born of the house of Vetori. Lorenzo is provided for, as my heir. He will die, if our luck holds, a king. Sebastian I shall put at the head of our navy—"

"Why, but, sir, but our little Melphé has not any navy," says Cesario, in some unavoidable if inept astonishment.

The Duke smiled. In his heavy gray face, it was like a smile lightly scratched upon iron.

"We shall have a navy in due time, do you depend upon it." He continued,—

"And Carneschi of course remains in command of my army for the present."

Cesario noted that odd phrase "for the present"; but he most wisely said nothing about it.

"—So that altogether, Cesario," the Duke summed up, "I have no special need of you. And for my own part, I would prefer, but for Carneschi, not to deny you your share of happiness in this world, so long as that happiness need not after all interfere with my plans for the future of Melphé. If I had married"—the Duke cleared his throat—"if I had married that dear dead soft-handed girl whom you praise with such eloquence, I would not ever have reigned in Melphé. I am not sure, mark you, that I would have been the happier. I have not observed that, in the long run, love matches turn out better than do marriages of convenience. Yet I do elect now and then, like an age-stricken dotard, to play with the notion of what my life might have been if Carneschi had not re-ordered my life."

He took up the goblet at his elbow and sipped temperately. It was the sweet wine of Tokay which he drank, yet the Duke's face was that of one who has just swallowed a most bitter but wholesome medicine.

"However!" he continued, "Carneschi, as I was saying is not bothered by any such notions. Carneschi will not hear of your marrying this Greek girl. Carneschi, I must tell you, has already planned suitable matches for each one of you. And Carneschi has arranged that you, my so eloquent Cesario, shall marry one of the younger princesses of Calabria. There are three of them to choose from, but they will probably palm off on you the hunchback. A younger son must take what is given him in the shape of a princess and be thankful. Her name is Joanna, I believe, if that matters."

"How much longer, sir," a despairing Cesario asked, "need this patriarchal lean heretic be our dictator?"

The Duke said, coldly: "I dispute the terms of your question. They imply that, through some inconceivable riot of ingratitude, I of my own accord might part with a revered friend to whom I owe all that I possess or may be to-day."

The boy spoke with conviction, saying: "Yet you have seen the proofs of his life-long treachery. Oh, sir, but you should have preserved them! They involved his eternal disgrace, his death even. They would have released you forever from this horrible old rascal who wants to marry me to a hunchback, and to ruin my whole life just as he has ruined your life."

"I must dare to question—now—if at your age, Cesario, you quite understand life. Carneschi has made me Duke of Melphé, through some double-dealing with me as well as with other persons. And the inconvenient evidence as to these facts I have, as a matter of course, given him to destroy. It was a courtesy which I owed to the usefulness, if not exactly to the unrestrained loyalty, of my chief servant."

"Of your chief servant! That, sir, is it, precisely; and I myself could not have expressed it with more exactness."

"You flatter me indeed, Cesario."

"—For in making you our Duke, sir, Carneschi

has raised you from the position of his pupil to the rank of his master, if you but dared to assert yourself."

"You are not pre-eminently polite, Cesario; yet you speak the exact truth. How, then, would you advise me to deal with Carneschi?"

"I would have him killed before the sun rises to-morrow," the boy replied, without any least hesitation, "for he has deserved it."

At that, the Duke openly chuckled.

"I shall duly weigh your advice"—gray Ferdinand promised,—"if only because it entertains me a great deal. I would but remark that to dispose of a prime-minister in the offhand manner which you have suggested, is not customary in high diplomatic circles."

"You conceive, sir," Cesario continued, resolutely pressing the main point at issue, "I do not wish to marry a hunchback. I wish to marry Hypolita. And you, if you so willed it, you could have this so infernally all-meddlesome, match-making servant of yours beheaded within the next half-hour, without the least bit of trouble to anybody. It is you who are the Duke, not Carneschi. He is nothing, except at your pleasure. You have merely to speak."

But still the Duke shook his large gray head, with a most regrettable obstinacy.

"No, Cesario: no, it is not right for a reigning prince to abandon and to destroy his best friends except upon high moral grounds or at some exceptionally good price. So I shall not speak. By ill luck, I have no military genius; and, indeed, battles frighten me. I am a physical coward. I need this Carneschi, who has not his living equal as a soldier, to continue in his command of my army. I cannot afford to lose him. I cannot even afford to cross his desires in anything."

"No, not, as you remarked just now, sir, not for the present," said Cesario, boldly.

Duke Ferdinand looked at him meditatively. The Duke's gray face displayed no emotion. He said, dryly:

"You observe trifles, Cesario. It is a useful accomplishment."

The boy asked, with a new and conspiratorial sense of comradeship:

"Well, and what follows, sir? I mean, of course, —for the present."

"It follows that as a private person, I do not disapprove of your marriage. I will even promise you to further it when once I am free to do so, should that ever prove possible. Yet as a reigning prince, I reply that—for the present, Cesario,—you cannot hope to marry this girl."

"I quite understand, sir. I cannot have Hypolita until you have a new prime-minister. And when will that be?"

"Time, let us hope, will answer your question, Cesario, with a frankness such as is not permitted to mere princes," replied the Duke, imperturbably. "Meanwhile, in your place, I would return to Gratignolles and resume my love-making, which at your age you ought to find somewhat more entertaining than are these dull routine matters of statesmanship."

Cesario said, "In this, sir, as in all other matters, I obey you with an entire heart."

V

Cesario thus left behind him, for that while (in the words of Barnacus), "the infrequent spectacle of a reigning prince who repaid his debts willingly;

for the titles, the manors, the pensions, and the yet
other emoluments bestowed upon Carneschi continued to evince the sincerity of Duke Ferdinand's
gratitude; nor did the resplendent benefactions
which the Duke now heaped upon the Huguenot
statesman abate in their munificence until after
Carneschi had overrun and conquered the adjacent
republics of Pania and Ferrata, with merciless and
inflexible barbarity."

The territory of Duke Ferdinand, in this manner, was not merely tripled. It had been rounded
off handsomely into a compact state, with stout
forts to strengthen the defences already prepared
by nature at every frontier,—except, to be sure,
where his lands touched the duchy of Bracciano.
An alliance with the Orsini, however, was well
under way. Ferdinand now desired no more con-
quests, but only to develop the snug kingdom procured for him by Carneschi.

"All that I have," said the Duke, frankly, "I owe
to you, my protector and life-long friend. My indebtedness I have endeavored to discharge as I best
might, but it now occurs to me that I can, moreover, make you Marquess of Ferrata and Lord of
Pania."

"Come, highness, you are far too prodigal," said Carneschi.

"To the contrary, my lord marquess,"—replied the Duke, smilingly—"I am just. I lament only that your advancement must necessarily halt with these titles, and that to repay you yet more generously is beyond the power of a mere Duke of Melphé."

Carneschi too smiled at that, saying, "Have patience, your majesty! for I shall make of you a king in due season."

Ferdinand answered, trustingly: "I believe you, my friend. Meanwhile, I can make you a marquess."

And this he did, with great splendor. It was indeed upon this same occasion that Ferdinand instituted the most noble Order of San Antonio; and nominated his so called prime-minister, but his actual master, to be the head of a knighthood of which the three declared objects were: to destroy the pirates of the Mediterranean; to liberate all such Christian prisoners of these pirates as were not Protestants; and to propagate in every kingdom the Catholic faith. Only after Carneschi had declined this honor, upon the ground that he happened to be a Protestant, did Ferdinand, with a confessed sense of diffidence, venture to assume it himself.

Having thus nobly shown his gratitude as a person and his equity as a prince, the Duke was now able to respect his conscience as a son of the Church. The newly created Marquess of Ferrata was therefore arrested, within twenty minutes after his investment; and during the same month of July he was delivered to his life-long enemy, Pope Pius, as a refractory heretic.

For his piety Ferdinand received an exceptionally good price, inasmuch as early in August the Pope published a bull confirming the possession of Ferrata and of Pania to Ferdinand and to his heirs forever; and allowing him (as being now the properly legalized overlord of all three of his stolen provinces) to assume henceforward a more resonant title, as King of Melphé.

VI

Kingship was an advancement of which the Duke of Melphé's formal assumption was delayed awkwardly. Carneschi, immediately before his departure in fetters, had arranged an excellent match for the Duke's older daughter (whom the Cardinal of Amboise was thought to have begotten for him), through betrothing this blonde, beautiful young girl to the sole son of the Lord of Bracciano. But now, no sooner was all settled satisfactorily, than word reached Duke Ferdinand that Madonna Beatrice was holding secret meetings, after night-fall, in a laurel grove to the rear of the Governor's Palace, with young Malandrino, captain of the Duke's body-guard.

Ferdinand at once summoned the rash couple to his private closet. With an unangered disapproval he rebuked them for conducting their liaison so clumsily, and he ordered Malandrino to prepare for immediate imprisonment. The young man went away sulkily, and even with some expressions of open discontent, toward his dungeon. But Madonna Beatrice flung herself at the Duke's feet, appealing for mercy, and declaring she could not ever marry Paolo d'Orsini, whom she found detestable.

"My child," said the Duke, mildly, "I admit that your betrothed is not remarkable for his good looks or his polished manners. But he is the heir of Bracciano and Anguillaria and all the lands around Civita Vecchia. An alliance with Bracciano ensures peace for the borders of Melphé. So of course you must marry him."

"But it is Malandrino whom I love—and whom I have loved unreservedly."

Up went the Duke's hand in quick protest.

"About your lack of reserve, my dear, I prefer to know nothing. Yet your love I can well understand, for Malandrino is a fine young fellow. I myself like him extremely. But I like better an alliance with Bracciano."

Then the sobbing desperate girl told him she was with child by Malandrino. The Duke did not move for an instant. He asked, by-and-by, how far advanced was her pregnancy? When she had answered him, he opened her gown to inspect her breasts. Afterward the Duke said:

"This is remarkably vexatious. Whether we go through with the match, or whether we break it off, at this late date, we shall have insulted Bracciano most flagrantly. And Melphé is not prepared for another war. Go to your rooms, my poor child. A priest will be sent to you at once. Do you pray with him for the forgiveness of your carnal offences, which have come so near to upsetting the welfare of two principalities, and for the ultimate salvation of your soul, my dear daughter, until I come to you."

The girl whispered, tense and gray, "Must I die, sir?"

"How else," asked the Duke, reasonably, "can I prevent a war in which regiments will die? Should you live on, after having got yourself in this state —through I cannot imagine what strangely shocking disregard of your maiden morality, as well as of the most simple physical precautions,— why, then, it would mean war for Melphé. So I must save many lives at the cost of one life. Who, my unfortunate dear child, would deny this course to be sound economics? or who, in fact, would deny the minor sacrifice to be a matter of plain duty, upon both our parts?"

She did not answer; nor is it known certainly just how her entrance into eternal life was arranged. But an announcement was made, on the following morning, that Madonna Beatrice had died, suddenly, of the malignant spotted fever.

She was buried by her grieving father with much splendor. Even the white mules which drew her white catafalque toward the Cathedral of San Marco were shod with silver. Her younger sister, Isabella, was then married to Paolo d'Orsini; and peace having been thus happily ensured for all the frontiers of Melphé, Ferdinand was now at liberty to proceed toward Rome. He there witnessed, with unruffled dignity, the punishment of Carneschi, during the feast day of St. Remigius. Upon the ensuing day, among ceremonials even more handsome and impressive, Ferdinand dei Vetori was consecrated, and was crowned King of Melphé, by the Pope's own hands.

His Holiness, it is true, in giving away Ferrata and Pania, had assumed the prerogative of the Emperor, to whom both these provinces had been subject nominally. But here again did the marital broad-mindedness of gray Ferdinand serve him to precision. The Emperor, out of his fondness for Prince Sebastian (whom, it may be remembered, the Emperor was supposed to have begotten upon Ferdinand's wife), said smilingly:

"It is quite fitting that my son should pass as the son of a reigning monarch. Moreover, neither Pania nor Ferrata has paid us any tribute for these last ten years. Besides that, I am at odds already with the Lutheran princes here at home, and at open war with the Turks abroad. To conduct three wars at the same instant would be highly inconvenient. Let us humor the gray pimp!"

[42]

Thereafter the Emperor Maximilian, by the grace of God, ever Augustus, Emperor of the Romans and King of Hungary and of Bohemia, despatched a fervent letter of congratulation to his illustrious friend and beloved cousin, Ferdinand, by the grace of God, King of Melphé, Prince of Ferrata, Duke of Fiena, Duke of Pania, Marquess of Tombay, Count of Alcarses, Count of Bescaglia, Lord of Serli, Lord of Arvieto, &c., &c. Ferdinand's titles were beyond counting nowadays.

Sweden, Naples, and Spain alone, for some little while, deferred in acknowledging the new monarch; all the other Continental powers concurred in felicitations; and the qualms of Duke Ferdinand's conscience as a sound churchman, in this salutary fashion, flowered with a king's crown.

PART TWO: THE LOVE OF CESARIO

VII

Now King Ferdinand prospered; and in this respect his realm tendered him the loyal homage of imitation. Melphé rested at peace with the entire world. The affairs of Melphé were administered with clemency and with intelligence. To her citizens that was a huge novelty, and indeed a benefaction somewhat perturbing.

People could not understand a king who desired neither glory nor luxury. Ferdinand, it is true, had begun to make that collection of precious and semi-precious gems which afterward became no less famous than it was fatal. In adding to this, he was free-handed; he was even imaginative. But otherwise, his sole interest appeared to be in adjusting the machinery of his government so that it would run smoothly; and over this taskwork he labored, at all hours, as prosaically as any other mechanic.

The conquered territories of Pania and Ferrata

had been absorbed tranquilly, without molesting the age-honored unreason of their national customs, or the time-approved systems of what their citizens were used, in oratory, to describe as representative government. In these republics all patriots who had fought against the invasions and the destructiveness of Carneschi were now pardoned, upon a fair commercial basis of heavy fines, without being hanged or even tortured; nor was any official who to-day acknowledged the overlordship of King Ferdinand removed from his post. Instead, to each republic had been guaranteed freely, upon gilt-edged parchment, with a particularly large seal, the integrity of all its ancient rights as an independent sovereign state; and while nobody had any least notion as to what that might mean, yet an assurance of the firm maintenance of their state's rights soothed patriotism.

The common people of Ferdinand's triple kingdom, in brief, now that warfare ceased and taxes had been reduced, were a deal happier under the drab economies of the sedate usurper than they had been under the more expensive heroisms of their legitimate masters. The merchants enlarged their shops. So marked, indeed, was the general improvement of affairs that the more enterprising merchants now maintained each a private mistress or a fine boy, handsomely, in the manner of well-born persons. And the nobles, after King Ferdinand had executed four or five of them for peculation or malfeasance, or for some other old noble habit, began wonderingly to accept his fantastic demands that a public official should dispense the King's justice honestly.

In Melphé this was a new notion. To the nobility in general, as well as to the best legal opinion, it seemed like balderdash; whereas to the more wealthy lords it seemed like a knell: and yet it seemed, also, as familiarity accustomed his people to the flimsy régime and to the half-baked theories of King Ferdinand, to make for a sort of fallacious contentment.

VIII

This half shame-faced sort of not quite believed-in contentment extended as far as to Gratignolles, where, to begin with, Cesario had heard with some discomposure about his sister's death and about the thrifty exchange of Carneschi's person for a king's title. Cesario had inclined, just at the first glance, to disapprove of the gray tyrant of Melphé's exploits in, as the lad phrased it, the muddied byways of treachery and of cold-blooded murder.

But then, to the other side, the old gentleman had most faithfully kept his promise to Cesario; for here was the letter—very neatly signed, and sealed with the coiled serpent of the Vetori—in which Ferdinand, by the grace of God, &c., &c., requested that his beloved and honored friend, Earl Lysander, Lord of Gratignolles, &c., &c., should be pleased to give to Cesario the daughter of Lysander in marriage. Cesario had faced a future so roseate ever since the arrival of this letter that, in his heart, he could not bring himself to regard its beneficent writer with one tenth of the abhorrence demanded by Cesario's judgment.

Nor indeed, as a highly complacent Lysander pointed out, ought anybody to judge a king's conduct by the criteria of a clodhopper. *Noblesse,* said Lysander—with the thoughtful air of a conscientious person who, in the self-same instant, needed to describe somewhat complicated matters with entire precision, and yet to avoid the uncolloquial and abstruse terms of pedantry—*noblesse oblige.*

Moreover, Lysander continued, one did try to retain the unbiased point of view of a scholar, even of the virtuoso, to whom life was a form of art. Æsthetically, at any rate, one could not but admire this fine pair of tragedies which King Ferdinand had contrived and had produced to perfection.

"But, Lysander," Cesario returned, with something like a sob, "but my sister's death is a grief to me."

Lysander said: "I submit to your better judgment, my prince, that one should not allow any such merely personal considerations to interfere with one's weighing of the performance as an artistic product. Your affection for your sister is, as I do not deny, commendable—within, of course, its own modest limits. But the great-souled father who decrees that his daughter should perish rather than survive dishonor is a notion truly majestic."

The boy replied, doubtfully: "Still, it is an old theme, Lysander. It is a theme without any æsthetic value, because—inasmuch as fathers have been killing their improperly punctured daughters ever since the days of Virginius—nobody nowadays could well write a first-class poem about any notion so old-fashioned."

[51]

"No theme, my dear prince, can survive long enough to become hackneyed unless it contents some eternal need of man's nature. It is the fond fault of youth to forget that whatsoever is trite must necessarily, for this same reason, be true."

"But—" says Cesario, a bit at sea.

"Moreover, King Ferdinand, like all other exalted personages, has to honor the naïve tastes of the public. Now, the public delights in just such sturdy stern moralities as is that of the father who ranks duty above his natural human affections. It delights equally, I admit, in the notion of the father who bids duty go to the devil because of his natural human affections; but the principle stays the same."

"Still—" says Cesario.

"The sudden tumbling down of Carneschi from his pre-eminence," Lysander went on, "was even better art, from all popular standpoints. His tragedy was well staged, with just the required touch of gaudiness."

"Now, but surely—"

"Not in the least," replied Lysander. "Carneschi was dressed most strikingly, in a long robe of yellow baize with a vivid large green cross embroidered on the front of it. Upon his head they had placed a tall cap painted with flames and devils; in his hand they compelled him to carry a huge lighted taper of green wax; and as he went by, with such graceful leniency was the affair conducted, the populace were not allowed to throw stones at him, but only handfuls of horse-dung and of human excrement, as a sign of his having been expelled from the body of the Church."

"I," said Cesario—who, like all boys of his age, had a kind heart when he happened to think of it—"I advised his extinction. Yes; I most strongly urged King Ferdinand to separate the gold of Carneschi's spirit from the dross of his body by means of the acid of death. Yet I would have permitted this scheming match-maker to die among fewer insults."

"You quite miss the point, my prince. The effect, doubtless, was crude and even malodorous. But it was sound popular art, because nothing more deeply pleases the public than to behold the downfall of a superior person. How then, and with what magnanimity, must the public have rejoiced to observe a great nobleman, a man of undoubted genius, converted into this stinking helpless figure

[53]

of fun! Your father has begun his reign with a fine act of philanthropy. Through this friendly appeal to democratic instincts, and to the plain man's congenital loathing of superior talents, he has made sure of King Ferdinand's popularity among the great body of his people everywhere."

"That is perhaps true," says Cesario, who was now, by the dictates of reason, somewhat shaken in his disapproval of the King's conduct. "Yet in this deplorable condition, Carneschi was compelled to ride slowly, upon the back of a mule, into the plaza, and he was there exhorted to repentance by a Dominican friar, who preached to him for more than an hour about his torments to come, both in this world and in hell. That, I submit, was excessive. Loving-kindness is handsome in its place, but sixty-five unmitigated minutes of it must have been tedious for everybody concerned."

Again Lysander stood ready to defend a king who was now about to make the daughter of Lysander a king's daughter-in-law.

"It was not at all tedious, my prince, for a devout populace who meanwhile could be looking at a pope, and a king, and cardinals by the dozen, and the Grand Inquisitor, and the Attorney Gen-

eral of the Holy Office, and so many other sancti-
fied persons, all in their robes of state and accompanied by the fine whores with whom they sleep.
You forget also the sadly tolling bells, the waving
banners of crimson damask embroidered with the
black and silver shield of St. Dominic, the flaring
torches carried by the friars, the green cross above
the improvised altar, and the huge black swaying
crucifix, with its tortured Christ, presiding over
His elect followers in this world, while they were
cutting off Carneschi's ears and castrating him.
No; there are few spectacles more inspiring to the
sincere Christian than is an auto-da-fé; and it is
not right of you, as a professed lover of the pic-
turesque, to disapprove of your royal father for
having contrived a pageant so handsome."

"Still—" said Cesario.

"Moreover, my prince, there is not any far-see-
ing patriot anywhere in Melphé who does not
applaud your father for having exalted Melphé
from the rank of a duchy to the status of a full-
fledged kingdom. The fact has been appreciated,
most volubly, by all public speakers and by dem-
agogues of every degree, that in order to serve his
country your great-hearted father did not hesitate

to surrender his best friend and main benefactor to a rather painful form of extinction. The dignified composure, and indeed the approving complacency, with which, at the conclusion of these surgical diversions, the King saw that which was now left of this heretical Carneschi incompletely garroted, and then burned at the stake while still alive, has been commented upon favorably by the very best people. Nor is there any pulpit in all Melphé from which King Ferdinand has not been praised as a most gratifying exemplar of sound Christianity."

The boy said: "I myself did not love Carneschi beyond the reasonable extent of my duty as a Christian. But I do not love, either, the thought that he was thus very slowly and horribly butchered in order that Duke Ferdinand might have a new title."

"Yet these religious exercises have procured for you also a new title, my prince. They have made you, as the son of a reigning monarch, the most desirable of my daughter's suitors. Otherwise, you conceive, it would have been my paternal duty to prefer Pescaro, whose grandfather has such a fine lot of old pagan manuscripts," Lysander said, half-regretfully; and concluded,—

"I deduce that you ought both to love the memory of Carneschi and to regard with lively gratitude that expiation of his heresies which has bought you your happiness."

"Why, but indeed, sir, unhappiness cannot well exist in the presence of Hypolita."

The boy spoke truthfully, so far as went his own view of affairs. It is possible that Lysander, as the father of Hypolita, regarded the girl somewhat more prosaically; but he did not dissent, in speech at any rate, because Lysander also, in his by-gone day, had been a fond lover.

IX

The Lord Lysander was of Grecian birth, they record, and in the days of his youthfulness he had served under the Duke of Athens. It was in this city Lysander had married his now deceased wife, upon the same evening that his overlord, as a fourth venture into wedlock, espoused a queen of the Amazons. The Duke had discarded this noble lady, in no long while, so that he might marry,

upon various occasions, a few other ladies, no whit
less noble, such as the Princesses Anaxo, and Peri-
bœa, and Iope, and Phædra, and Helen, and Phere-
bœa. But Lysander, who was of a less expansively
amorous nature, in addition to being unprivileged
by any such high rank as justified these matrimonial excesses, had remained moderately faithful
to the small sharp-tongued wife of his youth,
throughout three entire years. She had died then,
leaving him the invaluable loud legacy of two infant daughters.

They were called Hypolita and Hermia: and
with these girls, who now approached maturity,
the sedate Lord Lysander lived upon the Island of
Gratignolles, giving over his middle life to tranquillity and to study and to an impoverishment of
his modest estate through incessant additions to his
library.

For he delighted equally in old manuscripts and
in facetious new books and in the abstruse talk of
learned persons, to whom his house was as their
own home. Indeed, Lysander had with him at this
very time a most notable scholar, called the Sieur
de la Forêt, whose special forte (so Lysander told
Cesario) was omniscience. But above all, was the

island home of Lysander overrun with ardent young gentlemen who were in love with his daughter Hypolita.

Of these, Lysander now dismissed amicably the Vicomte of Puysange, the Count of Pescaro, and the Lords of Val-Ardray, Basardra, and Gontaron. Any one of these would have been an acceptable match; and Pescaro, in particular, would inherit that fine lot of ancient manuscripts about which Lysander thought wistfully even in the same instant that his common-sense conceded the superior utility of a king's son as your own son-in-law.

X

"Nevertheless," said the Sieur de la Forêt, just after he had finished explaining about the first Roman postal system as it was instituted by Augustus—and had so been forced to distinguish, in a rapid but pithy manner, between the government of the imperial provinces and the ten senatorial provinces of the Roman empire,—"nevertheless, friend Lysander, this Cesario is a minor poet. You cannot make out of a minor poet a satisfactory husband except through a year-long, steady massacre of his more noble ideals, of his shiftless high-hearted magnanimity, and of his slender talents. The demolition is not uncommon; it is indeed the restive, hurt heart of your human solidarity; or, to change metaphors, it is the missing arc which by-and-by rounds out to perfection most home circles. It is an assassination in which every capable woman revels; the clergy, the banker, and the police, regard it with approval; but me, I confess, it revolts."

"Friend and deluder of so many minor poets," replied Lysander, smiling, "you must promise me not to befriend and delude my Cesario. You must spare me my ewe lamb."

"Yet he would do rather well in Branlon—as you ought to know, Lysander, since it was you who, somewhat anciently, went into yet another enchanted forest near Athens."

"I did give way to such imprudence, Lord of the Forest; and nobody denies it. I entered that magic wood as a bachelor; I came out of it excessively married. So let us speak of more pleasant matters."

"Your slightest wish, Lysander, is my supreme law. I was only saying that I fancy the absurd youngster."

"So do I," returned Lysander, with the naïveté of learned persons, "now that his father is King of Melphé. That is why I must entreat you not to be misleading Cesario into any sort of high-pitched and high-priced woodland happiness. You conceive, Lord of the Forest, that with a prince as my son-in-law, I can get all the books I really need."

"Books, always books!" said Messire de la Forêt. "Well, I have no large quarrel with books. Yet I cannot but lament that, nowadays, they only should be your staid poor solaces, my poor Lysander, for the lost wonders which, very long ago, you observed in King Oberon's fine, moonlit forest. And I consider your declension to be doubly tragic because it is far too familiar. To each one of you who in your youth are poets it is granted to live among many magics. For that tinsel-gilt brief while, how very wonderful is each young poet! how far then, in his own nature, does the lad exceed mere magic! inasmuch as at every instant, how nimble and how unpredictable, how various and how fertile, is he in begetting, for the philosophic onlooker, an amazed amusement! His life is pure fantasy."

Afterward Messire de la Forêt said: "But as the

prime of his youth passes, even so his absurdity dwindles; it desiccates: and his rich bright vein of unconscious humor begins to run more and yet more tricklingly. He becomes infected, in short, by that which you mortal beings are pleased to describe as sanity; and on account of time's skulking counsel, he abandons the moon-colored oriflamme of romance. He quits the enchanted forest of Branlon. And I permit it. Indeed, I dismiss him of my own choice, because he is not fit any more to posture in divine Branlon, now that his foolishness has taken on a more solid and sordid cast."

Messire de la Forêt sighed then.

And he said likewise: "Yet after leaving Branlon, the time-ruined poet is very quick to deviate, not merely into marriage, but into every other sort of prosaic consolation for his lost splendors. He collects bank-notes and receipted tax bills and large dusty acres of building lands; or, possibly, he attempts to drug his vain regrets for Branlon's magnificence by keeping his small, snug shop well swept. It may be that, far more ambitiously, in the uniform of a captain, he tries to sweep clean the face of Earth itself, through disinfecting it of his fellow creatures with sword and musket; or perhaps, he labors toward very much the same end by setting up as a physician. At yet other times, my strayed servitor may seek to hide his failure under the silken robes of a judge, or of an emperor, or of a clergyman, or even of a most notable professor, in some famous college, expounding, upon weekdays only, to the inexperienced the untruthful."

Then Messire de la Forêt said also: "At all events, he descends by-and-by into the smug degradation of being highly esteemed by his better-thought-of neighbors. But let us not speak of that! Here, for the minor poet, is a downfall than which not even the untrammeled imagination of a demigod can conceive anything more dreadful. My friend, this is a ruining from which our so absurd, so young, and so pathetic Cesario will be no more able to escape than you could escape it. No one of you doomed minor poets can avoid your final subjection by time and common-sense, except through the but too sadly unfrequented avenue of an early death. Well! and for these reasons, Lysander, I at least would not grudge to Prince Cesario his transient small hour of young happiness, in my Branlon, before his inescapable doom has struck down this pompous boy, and has left him wallowing forever in the gray dust of respectability."

"But I would grudge it," Lysander replied, with decision—looking up from the book in which he had been reading all this while,—"because, to begin with, it was an enchanted forest which got me over well married; and because in the second place, I need many books; and because in the third place, it is my paternal duty to see to it that my daughters marry suitably. So now if only I can make a match of it between Pescaro and Hermia, why, then I can have all his grandfather's fine manuscripts too."

Messire de la Forêt shrugged.

XI

Of the two daughters of Lysander, the younger, to the extent of some eighteen months, was Hermia. She was likewise the smaller, the more disposed to quietness; and the good looks which she possessed in a reasonable degree were of an elfin cast. Hypolita was the beauty. To Cesario's finding, indeed, there was no beauty, anywhere, in any way comparable to the beauty of Hypolita.

"One may not find in any court a queen, or in any fairy tale a princess, or in any mythology a goddess," said Cesario, "whose splendors are not in comparison a mere drabness."

"That is foolish talk, my prince," says Hypolita; but without any other special sign of disapproval.

"I agree with you, my dearest," returned Cesario, after a moment of fair-minded consideration; "and as always, you are right. The poor creature, when compared with my Hypolita, would not appear drab. She would appear blackened, like an eclipsed sun."

"No," says Hypolita, smiling.

"As black," says Cesario, firmly, "as the raven's wing, or as smut, or as the ace of spades."

"How wonderful it is of you, my beloved," remarks Hypolita, in rapt admiration, "to think of so many comparisons so quickly!"

"As black as jet, or as ebony," went on Cesario, exceeding well pleased with her and with himself also. "As black as that ink with which some day, O my heart's treasure, I shall make your adored name immortal."

"I love all your poems," she replied, dutifully.

"As black as coal-dust, or as midnight," he continued.

"Or as a future without you and your dear nonsense, my poet lover," the girl hazarded, shyly.

At that, he kissed her hand fervently; and he said,—

"As black as that ugly mole on the cheek of Puysange, or as the scowl of Pescaro, or as the hair of the Sieur de la Forêt."

"Let us not speak of that evil creature," said Hypolita, shivering. "I do not believe him to be human. He is horrible. He frightens me, and I shall not ever be easy in my mind until he has left Gratignolles: for nowadays it is as though my dear father were attended by a tall devil."

"Well, but it is a learned devil," replied Cesario, tolerantly, "who speaks with a varied eloquence. I was no less interested, this very morning, by his exposition of the Pythagorean theory, that the entire universe has its origin in geometry, than I was in his lively description of the Scots legal process of recovering unpaid debts by letters of horning. He explained very clearly how cloisonné ware is made, and he gave a most excellent recipe for salting down fresh pork. The funds of his scholarship are considerable. And moreover it is a handsome devil, with curling fine hair as black as Satan's own heart. Do you not think so?"

The worshipful, fond girl answered that with a sweet directness:

"I do not think any man to be handsome except only you, Cesario. And please do not tell me about how black anything else is. I am not a great poet like you, my all-wonderful and all-gifted prince: and so, just sometimes, your cleverness does rather make my head ache."

"Hah!" says Cesario, disconcerted into a monosyllable.

"But even then," Hypolita added, "I love hearing you talk."

She was wholly adorable, the boy reflected, in this mood of dear candor. It seemed strange that, while he had duly praised in his verses her eyes, her hair, her feet, her bosom, her thighs, and all other such physical possessions as modesty permitted, and though he had hymned likewise her graciousness, her chastity, her loving-kindness, her bravery, and her yet other virtues, he had made no song about her unusual truthfulness.

XII

And so, when the sun had finished that day's
husbandry, leaving the wide fields of heaven well
sowed with stars; when careful night, ever mindful
of moths, had spread out her black robes far overhead for a wholesome airing; and when the chemis-
try of twilight had compounded the full moon,
like a silvered liver pill, to purge the sky of all dark
humors: even then did Cesario (after concocting
these special figures of speech) go about construct-
ing his poem.

Seated among oleanders, beneath the windows
of his adored lady, he rhymed now of how the most
pure and brave and most rare of the cardinal virtues, Truth, had ascended, from out of her proverbial well, into the false world of mankind, bearing
the sweet name of Hypolita. This advent, the boy
fabled, had awakened a worshipful despair among
all male persons who beheld her; and who necessarily perceived themselves to be too grimy to
merit in any way her kindly regard.

What muddy-natured male person anywhere,
indeed, could hope to merit the condescensions of

[68]

his immaculate Hypolita? the lad demanded of the
full moon. In attesting the question to be rhetori-
cal, and therefore unanswerable, the myths of four
pantheons were drawn upon; gems and flames,
along with the arrows of Cupid, the shears of Fate
and the science of botany, were all granted their
customary prominence, as the embroideries of Cesario's inability to reply to his own query. His
verses, in fact, were taking shape handsomely when
the flow of his poetic afflatus was broken by accident.

The accident was that he now observed Hypolita
above him, at her opened window, from which she
was letting down a rope-ladder to the dimly seen
person who waited below. Cesario did not move at
all in the while that this man ascended the ladder
and entered the bedchamber of Hypolita. It was
either Pescaro or Gontaron, Cesario knew, because
of Hypolita's other lovers, Puysange was corpulent,
whereas both Val-Ardray and Basardra were short
in stature.

Meanwhile Cesario considered himself with deep
interest.

"I do not feel the agony, or the hot anger either,
which undeniably, in accord with every sort of tra-

dition, I ought to be suffering at this terrible instant. That is strange. I do not feel anything whatever. Death has touched chillingly some part of me."

And that, he reflected, that was a quite tolerable phrase. "Death has touched chillingly some part of me!" Yes, even though it were deficient in any very marked exactitude of meaning, that *cri de cœur* had its overtones, its superb implications, and in brief, its poetic value. Something might be made of that phrase, in the form of a sonnet.

"Moreover, this not unhandsome phrase reminds me of my immediate duty to kill both of them. Let us get it over with."

—Whereafter Cesario too ascended the rope-ladder.

XIII

Hypolita's bedroom proved to be a handsome apartment, the chief ornament of which was a vast gilded bed, having its pink curtains held back by six Cupids in a marked state of masculine unrest. Upon the plump edge of this bed—quite naked now, and smiling with serene majesty—sat no one of Hypolita's declared lovers. Here sat, instead, that notable scholar, the Sieur de la Forêt; and for his heroic stark figure, the recumbent, the opulently curved, the gold-tufted, and pink-and-white nakedness of Hypolita composed a lovely but discomposing background.

Well, and it was to Hypolita that Cesario first addressed himself.

"O faithless and corrupt she-wolf!" said Cesario; "O wicked and most wanton Hypolita! with what words may I describe the lustful, the abandoned, the swinish, and the execrable infamy into which you have now fallen, through the lewd desires of your infected, fair, sweet flesh?"

"Really, my dear prince," observed the Sieur de la Forêt, as the young poet paused for breath, "you begin badly. Your exordium is ill-chosen, if but because it partakes of the uncivil. And moreover, your style is turgid. It is excessively highflown. It is, in brief, callow."

"Sir," said Cesario, "I am a poet. My heart's one love has betrayed me; and upon this superb provocation my most horrible fate demands that I speak not unworthily."

—To which the naked scholar replied: "How

wonderful a possession is youth! How admirable is its gift to make dear its untamed self-conceit, and its ignorance, and even its brave, shrieking, braying blatancy!"

"Nevertheless, sir," Cesario insisted, "a merely pedestrian style would not harmonize with my circumstances. They demand emphasis."

"They would not demand anything of the sort if you truly loved me," said Hypolita, "or had any least consideration for my good name. But that is you men, all over!"

Cesario answered, to his heart's one love: "Unblushing traitress! O most wicked cockatrice! O lewd siren!"

She replied: "And there you go again! Really, Cesario, if you have not any better manners than to come here uninvited, through a window, at an hour so compromising, then you might at least show the decency not to come shouting. No properly behaved girl who prizes her virtue, you must permit me to tell you, can afford to have her bedroom turned into a school of oratory at this time in the morning."

Among persons so callous, it was really not possible for any poet to keep up his poetry. Cesario blushed; and not merely over the insensateness of his audience. Cesario coughed in a tone which partook of the apologetic.

"I admit," said Cesario, "that I intrude at a moment more or less ill-chosen. Yet my curiosity as to who had supplanted me was very strong. I could not have slept comfortably without knowing who he was. So I must needs follow after the swaggering, triumphant, bold copulator whom I saw climbing into your window almost openly. I had sat under that window adoring you for some two hours. I was making verses in praise of—of all droll themes—your truthfulness. Well, and here is truth indeed, the frank truth, the naked truth."

He flung back his head. The betrayed poet laughed bitterly. And upon a sudden he took fire with inspiration.

"Untruss!" he cried then; "strip, O you lying Cesario! and let us all three give honor to the unveiled goddess in her own honest liveries!"

In an instant Cesario was tossing everywhither his great-sleeved jerkin, his violet-colored doublet, his shirt, his gilt-and-violet shoes, and his trunk hose, so that he stood there—white and young and slender, above the bright pile of his shed clothing—

as naked as were the perfidious girl and her gravely smiling, dark companion in unfaith.

"A fine gesture," remarked Messire de la Forêt; "and yet surely, in the bedchamber of a gentle-woman, my dear prince, a hat would be thought superfluous—"

Frettedly Cesario removed that infernal and quite forgotten violet-plumed hat which had made him appear ridiculous; and with a vigor but little short of pettishness he flung down this hat before he resumed his heroic attitude.

"Here," he proclaimed, "here is truth; here is candor; here is definiteness. We have done with pretending, Hypolita, you with your virtuousness, as I with my poetizing. Now let us all pig together in veracity."

She had drawn about her the bedclothing, before his approach. She said, thus shielded,—

"And what nonsense do you plan now?"

"Not any nonsense so entire as a rape," replied Cesario, as he drew back the coverlets, and stood quietly regarding her. "And yet—"

His voice broke. His voice broke, with a harsh squawk of emotion which troubled Cesario. He had loved this fair naked animal with an all-worshipful adoration such as, he now knew, he would not ever feel again, toward anybody. Indeed it was a passion which, already, he could not quite clearly recollect, or even wholly believe in.

"And yet," says he, "how beautiful is your bared body, Hypolita! I had dreamed for a long while, and always in a sort of sacred terror, that by-and-by I would see you thus."

She said, without moving, and with a half yawn,—

"You dream too much, Cesario."

"In fact," he admitted, "I had dreamed of an unreal Hypolita, who does not exist anywhere. So I loitered. In my fond blindness, I did not perceive your true needs, I did not serve briskly your hot needs. For this reason you have chosen in my stead a more perceptive and a more quick workman. Hah, but I do not doubt your tall learned workman is well worthy of his hire."

The Sieur de la Forêt said: "I am male, she is female, my poor minor poet. You have reached the inevitable instant when the young poet discovers that every healthy young woman enjoys copulation, and that she itches for it just as ravenously as he does. The discovery shocks him. Indeed, he

[75]

cannot afford to admit his discovery, without blasting his future as a poet. So he compromises. He hides away his unfortunate discovery, to the very back of his mind, out of his full consciousness. But throughout the rest of his youth—rather pleasantly, as a trespasser in forbidden beds—he will take his profit out of that unacknowledged discovery. In brief, the matured poet is a deformed animal who goes through life always facing in at least two directions without any becoming sense of incongruity."

Hypolita said, gravely, "It seems to me, just the same, and poetry or no poetry, that when we have our clothes on, and copulation, as you call it, is not convenient, we ought to pretend that doing it is not quite nice."

"Why?" says Cesario, who was much interested by this naked, new Hypolita.

"Why, because to pretend that is more well-bred. It is more religious."

"I agree with you, dear lady," remarked the Sieur de la Forêt—as he selected an armchair and disposed therein his noble naked form, so as to continue the conversation in comfort,—"that the more important and high-minded aspects of this tabooed amenity are largely a matter of dress. Though indeed, as the learned Stangate has justly observed, every dogma of morality is but a sort of clothing for human despair. Our pronouncements about good and evil—in his not inapt phrasing—are but the penitential robes, the sackcloth, and the accompanying dry ashes also, of man's ignorance, and of his lean helplessness, in a universe which he cannot pretend to understand, but yet hopes to placate—"

"To the contrary, Messire de la Forêt," replied Cesario—who, as a minor poet, had no patience with any such unmagnanimous thinking,—"you forget, I submit, Ardericus and his far nobler analogue. All human morals should more suitably be described as the cassocks and the chasubles, the lawn sleeves, the mitres and the surplices, of man's worshipping heart's hunger to honor, and to serve worthily, his unseen Creator—"

Messire de la Forêt, however, was now shaking his dark head; and he declared, dubiously,—

"Yet Roderick of Lugano says—"

"Yes," cried Cesario, sitting down beside his learned rival, and raising an admonitory forefinger, "but how neatly has replied Matthieu de Lèvres—"

"Benthius, none the less—"

"He was but a sciolist, my dear Messire de la Forêt. The Diet of Othnar, quite properly, dismissed him—"

"Yet Bishop Amaury of Pau, my friend—"

"Of course, he did! And what happened to him," Cesario demanded—"not two months later? It was an outcome from which you can judge for yourself."

"Now, but whatever in this world," says Hypolita, yawning, "do the pair of you imagine you are talking about, while I lie here neglected and taking my death of cold?"

The Sieur de la Forêt replied: "We two scholars —who love the noble pleasures of controversy, my dear, with a fondness that we deny to women— why, we are now dividing the raw meats of biology with the sharp cleaver of philosophy. We are agreeing, under this thick pelter of erudition, that since we are both naked here, at your bedside, Hypolita, with the thick, rich, lecherous, harsh, ugly, juicy smell of you in both our delighted noses, there is no need to pretend that the mating of a man with a woman can have, in the eyes of any case-hardened deity, a more important, or indeed a more depraved aspect, than has the mating of a bull with a cow, or than has a cock's treading of a hen. The spectacle, when observed at the not unremote distance of Heaven from our humanly cobbled-up civilization —or so at least, philosophy suggests—must be virtually the same in all three rump-heavings. Are we to imagine that Heaven would so rigorously distinguish among buttocks as to bestow condonation upon one upturned posterior and condign punishment on another?"

Cesario said: "That may perhaps be the divine point of view. And to me, in my present nakedness, it appears tenable. Yet, with my clothes once on again, I must reassume a fit sense of decorum along with my shirt, quite irrespective of celestial common-sense or of an all-seeing Heaven's urbanity."

"My dear prince," cried the Sieur de la Forêt, "I must entreat you not to ascribe to Heaven any urbanity. Urbanity is a man-made virtue; it is indeed man's only armor against the wild finesse of his womankind and the great gaucheries of Nature."

"Be that as it may," Cesario responded, "with

my clothes on once again, I must bear in mind that hereabouts our code of morals is not heaven-like. And I hesitate, I admit, to flout our mundane conventionality. Technically, from all tellar standpoints, this naked girl here is dishonored. Epigeally speaking, my heart is broken. And every local demand of respectability requires it of my self-respect that I should be revenged upon both of you through one or another adventure in homicide."

"And all because you must needs come climbing into my window at midnight!" says Hypolita. "You ought to be ashamed of any such irregular conduct, Cesario, because otherwise we could have been married quite comfortably. Otherwise, as you must let me remind you, you would not ever have contracted these painful doubts as to my strict virtue. And at all events"—she added, yawning yet again, as she lay back in the gilded bed, and spread open her splendid naked legs,—"at all events, the insane pair of you would not now be talking me deaf and dumb and blind."

"No, the affair goes deeper than that," Cesario asserted, looking pensively at her parted legs. "It all springs from the fact that I was so romantic-minded, a mere thirty minutes ago, as to be composing a poem under your window. If I had gone prosaically to my bed instead of to your bed, at a suitably soon hour, not any of this confusion would have happened. I think that I shall compose no more poems, for it appears to be a recreation too costly."

But Hypolita was meditating as to far more practical matters, in the while she continued to lie on her back, scratching the inner side of her right thigh, reflectively.

"And what, Cesario," she inquired, of the pink-and-gold ceiling, "what will you say to my father?"

"There again, my dear," Cesario answered, "the virtues which go on and off with our clothes are a nuisance. If I tell him the truth, then he, being clothed, will feel it his duty to his honor to insist upon an immediate marriage between you and Messire de la Forêt."

"But, as it happens," said the latter, "yonder in Branlon I am already blessed, to the extent of all my fair requirements, by the insomnia of yet another wife."

"In that case, he will have to challenge you to

mortal combat, to a duel *à outrance*, as an unprincipled seducer."

"Yet he would thus ensure his own death, Cesario, leaving all other matters unchanged; and to do that would be simply silly."

"It would be indescribably silly, Messire de la Forêt. But well-bred persons, with their clothes on, have to consider the demands of honor; and the honor of his house will have been insulted."

"I think, myself," said Hypolita, "that it would be far more kindly of us all not to upset my dear father by annoying him with the truth. We ought to be unselfish, I submit, as to our own natural liking for candor; and be glad to make even the most unpleasant sort of self-sacrifice, by lying suitably, for the sake of his feelings."

"Upon the other hand," Cesario continued, reflectively, "if I tell him that for my own reasons I have decided not to marry you, then equally the honor of his house will have been insulted. He will have no choice save to challenge me for jilting his daughter; nor in the circumstances will I have any choice except to waive my superior rank, and to accept his challenge. We would have to fight *à outrance;* and since neither of us has any special

proficiency at fencing, it will be a ridiculous con-
flict, in which either my good friend Lysander or
I, or perhaps both of us, will be slaughtered."

Hypolita said: "So now you see! Now you can
see for yourself, Cesario, that it would be very
much the simplest thing, for us two to get married,
without bothering about honor and truthfulness,
and upsetting everybody's comfort, and getting
people killed."

"No," said Cesario. "In my nakedness, I can perceive the good sense of our doing that, just as
plainly as, now you are equally naked, I can perceive the solution would have its pleasant side: but
with my clothes on, I shall yet again become self-
respecting and high-minded; and in that straitened
condition, I could not promise to love, honor, and
cherish, a shattered ideal."

Hypolita sat up in the bed, and she pushed back
her bright loosened hair with both hands, somewhat indignantly.

"Why, then," says she, "we are simply getting
nowhere with so much eternal talking."

"Yet I have, I think, a solution," said the Sieur
de la Forêt, very smoothly. "The thought occurs to
me that, for Lysander's benefit, Hypolita ought to

discover her affection for the Count of Pescaro to be imperishable."

"Why do you drag in that impudent, lean, lewd, black-faced Pescaro?" Hypolita asked, with frank wonder.

"Merely, my child, in order that I may recall to you the highly convenient devotion of my predecessor in this bed last night."

Hypolita, flushing somewhat, replied, "I think you are utterly horrid."

"To be utterly horrid," agreed the Sieur de la Forêt, "is a trait common to many stainless characters." He continued:

"Whereas you, my prince, have only to note, still for our form-loving Lysander's benefit, that imperceptibly your affections have been transferred to his daughter Hermia. For that, you cannot, or at any rate you will not, be held to blame too severely. Love conquers all, you will remark, with a suitable embroidery of high language. It is a remark which many people with their clothes on accept as rational. You have, for the rest, your father's consent for you to marry the daughter of Lysander."

"Why, but, to be sure," says Cesario, stroking his smooth chin, "which daughter was not specified; for I doubt if the old gentleman knew their names, and certainly he does not care which one I marry."

"In this way," continued the Sieur de la Forêt, "all can be glossed over handsomely, since Lysander will still be getting his true desire, without any least affront to what people with their clothes on have to describe as the honor of his house. He will still be getting a king's son as his son-in-law, to buy for him a fine lot of books. And what is yet more to the purpose, he will be marrying off his other daughter to a fine lot of manuscripts."

"But I had far rather," said Hypolita, in frank ruefulness, "be married to a prince."

"That may well come about in time," the sublime, stark-naked scholar assured her, gallantly, "for you have immaculate beauty and much enterprise. Yes; now that I regard the future, I predict that of these two pre-eminent virtues, the first will ensure the devotion of some monarch or another, in due course,—whereas that second virtue, your superb quick enterprise, may be counted on to dispose of Pescaro the very moment that he becomes superfluous."

The girl looked at Messire de la Forêt, smiling

with a remarkable sweetness; the lovely naked shoulders of Hypolita moved slightly toward the pink-and-gold ceiling; but Hypolita said nothing.

Instead, it was young Cesario who now put forth the ripened fruits of deliberation, by saying:

"Moreover, I am fond of Hermia. I have no great desire to marry her, but even so, matrimony is more healthful than a duel *à outrance*. And besides, it is you alone, Hypolita, whom I have loved. So I must protect you from the consequences of your perhaps natural but none the less illicit behavior. Should I ask Lysander, with the proper amount of misrepresentation, to let me marry Hermia instead of you, I shall have properly shown my unswerving devotion to you. Moreover, I shall then have avoided considerable trouble, and perhaps death, for the three of us who sit here naked— and for Lysander also. Yes: that is the best, the truly philanthropic solution; and I shall transfer my affections immediately after breakfast. Meanwhile, I shall put on again my clothes, along with the pretensions that go with them; and afterward climb down your rope-ladder."

This angered Hypolita, as in the same instant

[86]

that Cesario was fastening up his codpiece, he was forlornly pleased to observe.

"But have you no jealousy?" says she; "and is it the part of a gentleman, to be leaving me here to be ravished by a naked man?"

"No," said Cesario, very quietly, reaching for his doublet; "but then I am not any longer a gentleman. I am a poet; and I have been betrayed."

XIV

Now Lysander likewise took the affair quietly.

"Love is a mighty lord," the time-ruined poet remarked, "as I have cause to remember with some unavoidable blushings. You have found at a good hour, Hypolita, that you love Pescaro. The Count is a most worthy young man, apart from a tendency to cheat at cards, and his worldly estate, howsoever curtailed at present, will be handsome when his grandfather dies."

"No, my dear father," Hypolita replied, "for we shall be very poor even then. Even then my beloved Marcello and I shall have to live upon our mutual adoration and an occasional crust in some modest cottage. But what does it matter so long as true love unites us?"

"Why, nothing at all!" Lysander agreed. "The course of true love, as I can remember remarking to your dear sainted mother during the days of our courtship, never did run smooth. And she agreed with me. She devoted, in fact, every moment of our married life to proving how right I was."

And Lysander sighed, reminiscently.

"However," he continued, "I was not talking about money. The true point is that the old gentleman, while not vulgarly wealthy with gold and bank-notes, managed, during the pious season of his crusading days as a pirate in the slave trade, to steal a most notable lot of manuscripts from our pagan enemies. Among them, I hear, are six books of Livy and the complete verses of Sappho. These he will, no doubt, bequeath to his heir. Why, but of course he will! his known integrity forbids me to think otherwise. So Pescaro has my blessing."

"And I, sir?" Cesario asked.

"The Sappho manuscript," Lysander answered, blissfully, "is reported to be unique. It is at all events well-nigh priceless."

"Yes, sir, no doubt; but no whit less priceless—

to me, at any rate, and as I have just now made bold to remark—is your daughter Hermia."

"Why, but to be sure! So you, my prince, desire Hermia? Then, do you take her. She is yours. Nobody can better understand these unavoidable changes of affection than I do, for I once suffered from them myself, in a wood near Athens. Now, the Livy is an Alexandrian copy, with some excisions"—Lysander added, regretfully,—"but in this world one cannot have everything."

"And in fact, sir," says Cesario, "it may be that Hermia will not have me."

"Let us not talk nonsense," replied Lysander. "My daughters have not ever crossed my wishes except in secresy since I first started thrashing them. Why, at this late day, should they be beginning any such impieties? Do you but notify Hermia of her good fortune, and I will warrant her Christian-like acceptance of it."

Cesario obeys; and young Hermia listens, provisionally.

THE KING WAS IN HIS COUNTING HOUSE

XV

He had found Hermia upon the northern beach
of Gratignolles, on the side of the island which faces
Poictesme. She sat there upon a fallen tree from
which time and the sea's waves had stripped the
bark, leaving it all a pale silvery gray color in the
sunlight. And Cesario rested beside her, observing,
as it so happened, the sharply cut blackness of his
own shadow, on the white sands, during the ten or
twelve minutes that he spoke with a convincing
and, indeed, heroic passion.

The beginning poet would have chosen, in view
of the day's heat, to have spoken in some other surroundings. His upper lip, for example, as he well
knew, was perspiring visibly; and in the while that,
with a casual light gesture, he brushed away these
sweat beads, Cesario regretted that his declaration
should of necessity have to be made in this place of
hot glaring sunlight. So much perspiration did not
at all fit in with true poetry.

Nevertheless, he spoke with some handsomeness,
as he could not but admit, during the brief résumé
that Cesario now gave of his long-hidden adoration,

and of the irresistible passion which had burst all bonds. He was acceptably desperate, without any crude flavor of ranting. His words were well chosen. He discovered his five introductory similes to be striking. He quoted Horace not at all inaptly, as to the timid fawn, assuring Hermia that neither as an asperate tigress nor a Gaetulian lion did the speaker now approach her. Even his own nicely critical ear found his loud groans to be gusty paragons of sincerity; yet how inadequate (as Cesario mentioned) were they, as mere tongue-tied witnesses to his interior ardor, and as the reporters of a conflagration such as Ætna and Stromboli and Vesuvius could not have paralleled if all three had been set ablaze in Cesario's breast! For (to conclude) how very far, and indeed how immeasurably, above the narrow and the weed-choked ways of her lover's untutored speaking, arose the perfections of Hermia, like a tier of shining balconies, upon which every Grace and each one of the major Virtues sat, in full view, striking dumb the beholder!

"Here are fine noises," replied Hermia, to this superb peroration.

"I think so, myself," agreed Cesario, "inasmuch

as the truth when simply spoken has always its own rustic eloquence."

"Truth spoke somewhat otherwise, Cesario, last night."

"And what does that mean, my all-worshipful small Sphinx?"

"It means," the girl answered, "that my bedchamber is next to Hypolita's bedchamber."

Well, and at that, her glib worshipper sat bolt upright upon the log for an entire half-moment of silence.

"So you listen at keyholes," says Cesario, with unhidden disapproval. "That is dishonorable. You ought, my dearest, to be ashamed of yourself."

"But I am not your dearest, because Hypolita is your dearest, and besides, what else was I to do? It was not fitting that my own sister should be having two men in her room."

"No, not at the same time," Cesario agreed, "inasmuch as the pious are forbidden to indulge in works of supererogation. So I do not wholly blame you for listening. And besides, it makes matters simpler. It shows you, I think, that you and I have no real choice except to marry, for your father will now insist upon it."

"The trouble is that I have always been somewhat in love with you," says small Hermia, thoughtfully.

"I did not know that, my dear," said Cesario, touched. He brushed off his upper lip again, preparatory to kissing her before long; and he said, comfortingly:

"Still, that is not any permanent obstacle. You will get over being in love with me, in almost no time, when once we are married. And after all, you may find me a so-so husband."

"Yet to the last hour of your life, Cesario, you will be loving Hypolita. But you will be hating her, too, for the hurt which she has done to your self-conceit; and your hatred will not ever give you any rest until after you have been revenged on her."

He regarded this romantic-minded grave young person quizzically. He smiled then, in frank self-derision, saying:

"You credit me, my dear, with epic passions which I do not possess. I am a mere fribble. There is no depth to me, either for good or—by the best of luck—such evil as you suggest."

"I think otherwise. And I think also that your wife will get no large chance of happiness, Cesario, because she will not ever have any husband. She will have only a spoiled tall baby to fret the woman's heart out of her. And yet for my own foolish reasons, I will marry you if you like."

"Why, then the end justifies the means," says Cesario; "and as my wife, you shall be at entire liberty to protect the world at large from my forever embittered and poisonous nature."

Thus speaking, he took a ring from his little finger, and he placed it upon the ring-finger of Hermia's left hand.

"With this ring, dear Hermia," says he, "I plight to you my eternal faith. With this ring I do here and now, without bothering any priest about it, take you to be my wife."

She replied, gravely, "With this ring, Cesario, I take you to be my husband."

"Moreover," he continued, "moreover, you common scold, I must point out to you that the vivid green stone in this ring—which I borrowed from King Ferdinand's fine collection when he was not looking—is a bezoar stone found in the stomach, or to be more precise, in the duodenum of a unicorn. It is a gem which turns red with the contact of any poison. Well! and it does not change when I touch it, you perceive; in consequence, my nature, howsoever abandoned, cannot be entirely envenomed. That, my dear wife, is what grave-minded persons call logic."

"That, my absurd poet, is nonsense. But the ring is very beautiful. And so are you."

He kissed her lightly, in consideration of the warm weather; and he said:

"Small elf, with the inquisitive quiet eyes, I begin to love you. I love your tranquil smiling over a secret which is not known to anybody except you alone. I love you because you are like a squirrel, which is untamed and soft and defenceless and tiny. I love you because of your astounding lack of good judgment in loving me. And last of all, I love you because of your inmost heart's contempt for Cesario. You do not trust this Cesario, upon whom has been laid the curse of Reuben. 'Unstable as water,' you remark, with some superficial sound sense, 'he shall not excel.' Nevertheless, I begin to love you, Hermia, in sober earnest; and I think that my love shall yet put all sorts of cool reasonableness to confusion."

"As if ever you could learn to be quite in earnest about anything, Cesario!" the girl answered, forlornly, "except only yourself and your phrase-making and your self-conceit!"

"Ah, but I now intend to take daily as well as nocturnal lessons in gravity," he reassured her, "from the most dear of all tiny teachers. I shall thus learn how to pull a long face over far more extensive fields of knowledge. Meanwhile, as you must let me repeat, I adore you, child; and with you to help me, I do not dread any devil, not even that lean, scoffing, paltry devil which is Cesario's small soul."

Then Cesario said: "I am a happy man; I am no true poet; for my love is all lovable. There is in my need of Hermia no resentment, no unease, no abjection. 'Behold, thou art fair, my love: thou hast doves' eyes.' In this manner did an old Hebrew prophet, sniffling through his fat long nose, prophesy as to my small Hermia. I had not ever understood his saying until this instant. Dear Hermia, but I am not worthy of this instant! It is not right you should love me."

And Cesario said likewise: "Yet since injustice triumphs, let us applaud our preserver. I have got utterly free of all doubt or sorrow now that small Hermia loves me. I shout the astounding news to

[96]

heaven. I pity the poor blessed folk in heaven, who have not any joy like my joy. I cry out my gratitude to that injustice which has made my contentment to be firm and everlasting. I praise in this manner that huge injustice through which I have been made more enviable than is any saint roosting up yonder."

The small woman replied with extreme quietness to this fervent and this too declamatory, tall child. And in the while she was speaking, Hermia stroked ever so lightly the back of his strong young hand, two or three times.

"Do you be still, O my absurd half-poet whom I half love. It is not sensible to boast under this wide, bright sky. The sky hears us, perhaps; and the sky is big and strong. But we are little. We are light frail creatures. We are like that pair of ospreys who float driftingly. Kiss me, Cesario, while our small happiness lasts, for yet one drifting moment longer, under this large sky which has not any cloud in it."

The boy obeyed his betrothed wife, with a frank bit of amused tolerance, perhaps, yet with frank affection. The young egoist was wholly happy. He knew that this sufficiently pretty and but slightly perspiring, tiny Hermia adored him. He knew that he liked the smell of hot seaweed. He knew that Cesario was utterly wonderful; and that, in fact, Cesario was the superior of all other humankind.

Then he said, affably: "But for a sober, married couple, my wife, we become unbefittingly high-flown. Let us avoid these excesses in the romantic, at any rate in so much hot sunshine. Let us composedly tell your father that the affair of our marriage is settled, for I perceive he approaches. So do you untwine, wanton! Do you spare your staid father's blushes, since his present mood is austere. He wears an uncommonly grave face; and he comes attended by a pair of clergymen. I infer that they intend to marry us all over again."

XVI

Far from that, the two clergymen knelt before Cesario, saying,—

"Hail, Eminence!"

The boy stared downward at their shorn, gray-fringed heads. His mouth trembled. On a sudden he felt young, and inexperienced, and very help-less.

"What *is* this mummery?" says he; "and since when was I eminent in the eyes of my ghostly fathers?"

"Ever since that moment," they replied, "when, four days ago, the Holy Father of all Christendom was pleased to entrust us with this letter."

Cesario read part of the letter. He said, in his bewilderment,—

"It appears truly that Pius, bishop, servant to the servants of God, after desiring for me health and the apostolic benediction, and duly weighing my known piety and his deep love for his well beloved son in Christ—"

The frightened boy broke off short. He cried out, sharply:

"But then, I cannot marry Hermia! Here is lunacy. What does this signify?"

They told him.

XVII

Now the tale which the two priests of St. Dominic related to Cesario, upon the hot sunlit beach at Gratignolles, ran in somewhat this fashion.

King Ferdinand (said they), being at his country residence near Bescaglia, and having with him his Queen, had been joined there by her two sons, Gratiano and Sebastian, both of whom had but newly arrived in Melphé at this time.

Sebastian, who was now Lord High Admiral of the Melphean navy, came from the Emperor's court, where the blustering young fellow had been received fondly by his reputed father, and was entertained with magnificence. The Emperor, for that matter, now proposed to marry Sebastian to the Emperor's own niece, the Archduchess Anna. It was known also that the name of Prince Sebastian would be presented, when the election diet next met at Warsaw, as the preferred candidate of Austria for the now vacant throne of Poland.

But Cardinal Gratiano came from Rome, where his stay had been not merely magnificent. It was triumphal. Never, said the pious and learned College of Cardinals, smiling over the handsome bribes tendered them by King Ferdinand, had their sacred ranks received a more profitable or brilliant recruit. Young Gratiano's strict notions as to fleshly continence had been talked about everywhere, for he maintained, as was well known, three very lovely and accomplished boys whose sole duty was to pre-

vent him from being led into any immoral conduct with women. Not every young clergyman—
as it was admitted, with frank regret, among his
confrères,—protected his personal virtue with so
great carefulness.

Pope Pius himself had pronounced Gratiano to
be "of mature judgment and wise beyond his years,
and of such ability that it would be impossible to
find anyone more attractive, more seemly in his
morals, or more sensible." The Pope openly favored
the Cardinal Bishop of San Marco as his successor,
in preference to the more venerable Cardinal Priest
of San Sixtus.

In brief, all prospered with the Vetori; and King
Ferdinand, in this effusive glow of success, had become genial. Though he treated his stout, good-
natured handsome wife with a continuing cool
politeness, he now smiled at Sebastian's rough-and-
tumble ways, whereas toward Cardinal Gratiano
the King displayed something like open affection.
So all fared pleasantly at Bescaglia, where people
hunted until sunset, and danced until the sun's
rising, and made love in between whiles.

They held a deer-drive in the forest; and when
the game was rounded up, then a notable full-

grown roebuck lightly escaped from the huntsmen and made off into the heart of the woods. The two princes of the Vetori, gay in green and scarlet, pursued this beast; and by-and-by saw the buck quietly grazing in an open space surrounded by gum-trees and large holly clumps.

Sebastian, who was in advance, motioned his brother backward, and raised his gun. At the same instant, Gratiano fired and brought down the game. Sebastian swore loudly, while Gratiano dismounted and ran forward to inspect his prize.

"But it was my shot, by rights," says the Admiral of Melphé, leaping to the ground, in a fine rage.

"Yet it is my roebuck," says the Cardinal of San Marco, unanswerably, "since I killed it."

Sebastian had out his hunting-knife, brandishing it.

"Lying priest! you smug half-woman! you back-door thief! you shall not swindle me."

"Oh, go to the devil," cried Gratiano, pushing him aside.

Sebastian struck.

It all happened very quickly. Gratiano lay beside the dead deer, with a great wound in his groin, spouting blood; and Sebastian was now staring at him in terror. Neither young man could quite believe in the evidence of his own senses.

Gratiano said: "May God forgive us both! Call help, my dear." And afterward spoke no more.

In a dazed whirl of panic, Sebastian sounded his hunting-horn wildly. Huntsmen, in the King's liveries of green and russet, came galloping, by twos and by threes, from every side of the glen, to find the young Admiral weeping over dead Gratiano.

A wide deal of confusion followed, with everybody behaving futilely. All was a hubbub of questions, of exclaimings, of oaths, of men jostling and debating with one another; then came silence. A horse whinnied in the sudden silence. You could hear only a thin rustling of leaves underfoot, as the huntsmen stood aside, bare-headed, to make room for the King and the Queen of Melphé.

"O God!" cried Queen Caterina; and began to blubber, loudly, without any dignity.

But King Ferdinand did not speak at all. He waited there, looking downward, as if in meditation, first at the blood-drenched body of Gratiano, then toward the sobbing desperate Sebastian, who lay half prostrate at the King's feet.

Of his wife's children the King regarded with
the least favor the frank and passionate Sebastian.
The boy had no great harm in him: but he blus-
tered too much; his speech tended toward coarse-
ness; his manners, in the light of those rumors as
to his birth, were untactfully imperial; nor was he
very intelligent. Sebastian could not well hope to
be King of Poland, because no matter what the
Emperor might prefer, yet in the end that throne
would in all probability go to the Duke of Anjou.
Sebastian, in brief, except as a possible provider of
heirs, now that Lorenzo's wife stayed disappoint-
ingly sterile, had been of no grave importance until
now.

He was now horribly important, because he had
killed Gratiano. In the amiable and accomplished
Gratiano—whom, moreover, Ferdinand believed to
be his own son, if that mattered—had rested the
assured welfare of Melphé. Gratiano's election in
due course to the Papal chair had been virtually
assured. With one of the Vetori king over Melphé,
and with one of them King of Poland (since that
outcome had always remained at least possible,
until to-day), and with another regnant as Pope,
and with your son-in-law now Lord of Bracciano,

you would have stability. You would have a firm
hold upon affairs. And all this had been settled. All
this had seemed to be arranged as unchangeably as
is the grave moving of a planet in its orbit, when the
young blond sobbing emperor's bastard, with his
daubed hunting-knife, had flung down the bright
future of the Vetori, along with his own possible
crown, along with a Pope's triple tiara, into the
same dustiness in which the boy now grovelled.

Ferdinand did not hurry about the unpleasant
task set for him. He moistened his dry lips, that was
all. He said:

"Your brother's blood demands vengeance of
God, and so of me, who am God's regent in Melphé. That which I do, Sebastian, I must needs
do."

The boy stared at him desperately; and young
Sebastian shuddered. Sebastian cried out,—

"Strike quickly, gray snake."

"Haste is unseemly," the King replied, "in the
performing of justice."

Then, baring his gray head, and spreading out his
arms toward a pallidly blue sky with no cloud anywhere visible in it, King Ferdinand invoked of God
the All-Father, in quiet and grave terms, his own

pardon as the instrument of Divine wrath. He spoke slowly, without any special sign of emotion.

But the Queen shrieked, "My son!"

"Conrad! Balthazar! Antonio!" the King answered, sharply, "do you assist her Majesty. She is faint. Support her by both arms. If it be necessary, gag her."

He was obeyed. They restrained her, stifling her screams with their ungloved hands. Conrad dei Guardini she bit fiercely, so that his fingers bled.

The King meanwhile continued to address Heaven, in a firm but respectful fashion, requesting eternal peace for the souls of Gratiano and Sebastian. He took up Sebastian's hunting-knife. He plunged it into the boy's breast.

Sebastian, still kneeling, grinned upward at his executioner rather horribly. Then tumbling backward, with a deep sigh, and lying asprawl, in green and scarlet, across the green-and-scarlet body of Gratiano, Sebastian died.

Only the King's mouth, as he gazed downward, with an air of remote compassion, had moved, somewhat. It was as if gray Ferdinand were trying to moisten his handsomely curved, thin lips, and could not quite manage it.

He turned toward his wife, saying with grave courtesy:

"Madonna, I regret that your day's diversion should have been thus interrupted. I take it that no one of us has much appetite for any further pleasure-seeking to-day."

"Gray snake!" she answered him, laughing. "Our poor Sebastian was no scholar. I must find words for him. I must seek out some more fit and more horrible terms for the great King of Melphé, for the stabber, for my son's murderer."

"There has been no murder done here," the King replied—"by anyone." He faced the perturbed huntsmen, saying:

"Gentlemen, I must make bold to remind you, one and all, that you yourselves have just witnessed the death of the Cardinal and of the Admiral from malarial fever. It may be rumored abroad that they died otherwise, for the world delights in slander, and envy is always nimble to defile the good fame of princes. I can but rely upon your witnesses."

All answered him, "Majesty, we have indeed witnessed that which you say we have witnessed."

"You are the more wise," declared King Ferdinand.

The Queen continued to laugh, now more and more loudly.

"Attend to her," the King ordered.

—Whereafter the King rode back alone to his hunting lodge, whence he despatched a letter to the Pope, written in the King's own hand, and sealed with the coiled serpent of the Vetori, asking that Cesario be named as Cardinal Bishop of San Marco in dead Gratiano's stead. King Ferdinand wrote steadily and smoothly, weighing each phrase; and he endured patiently, without any least visible sign of annoyance, his wife's screams and wild laughter in the next room, where two physicians attended her.

"The bitch whines somewhat loudly for her pups," he remarked, as he scattered sand upon his completed letter.

Afterward the King summoned three secretaries; and through their decorous aid, the deaths of Gratiano and Sebastian, from malarial fever, were made public in due form, as Ferdinand, by the grace of God, &c., &c., announced to the various monarchs of Christendom his paternal bereavement.

XVIII

So then did it come about that the Queen of Melphé lay dead upon a couch in her bedroom, for her coffin had not yet been prepared. And so, too, did it happen that the new Cardinal Bishop of San Marco now stood alone beside the corpse of his mother, in the throes of attempting an unbiassed observation of his own anguish, or at any rate, of his traditional grounds for anguish.

His grief was not satisfactory. As a child, Cesario had loved, and he had very fondly admired, this rather stout but still handsome woman—approaching her always with a certain sense of presumption, he reflected, because even in childhood one knew that she had been approached by so many other more famous and grown-up adorers, in far-away places which to the child were only names; but which the child none the less knew to be real places, like Arvieto and Serli, in which his beautiful mother (for very truly she had been beautiful then) had once lived in iniquity—after the high fashion of the Queens Morgaine and Semiramis and Cleopatra for example, in histories that had delighted the quiet, book-loving child,—and where

[109]

she had sinned gloriously with fine shining gentlemen, who were not like one's plainly clothed and
glum and unexciting father. It had cordially pleased
the child (he remembered) to know that Queen
Cleopatra also had borne a son called Cæsarion; because that was almost the same as Cesario. For him
to be recalling this trivial fact, at this exact instant, with his mother lying dead here before him,
appeared droll. Later, though, after reaching viril-
ity, he had thought at many times with distaste,
and even with a certain sense of jealousy it might
be, about the scores of men who had gone to bed
with his mother, upon one or another occasion.
Like Nero, perhaps, he had always been somewhat
in love with his jovial and sweet-smelling and handsome mother.

At any rate, even though it seemed to him a sad
thing that, within so brief a while after the deaths
of Gratiano and Sebastian, this greathearted, if perhaps rather gross creature should have died insane
and terror-stricken—calling out always, so they
told him, for her baby Cesario,—yet he was not
feeling a sufficient amount of anguish. Just as when
he found Hypolita had betrayed him, so here, his
emotions were not rising to the occasion with a

suitable fervency. He was sorry for his mother's death, and for Gratiano's death. He regretted Sebastian's death, also, more or less. At heart—as Cesario now noticed, with complete self-disapproval—he had at no time really forgiven Sebastian for beating and scratching Cesario so often during their shared boyhood; Gratiano and Lorenzo had not ever bullied Cesario, that far-away baby Cesario. Yes: he was sorry; but by rights he ought at this instant to be in a frenzy of sorrow, convulsed by an immense whirlwind of grief. In point of fact, now that he considered himself closely and yet more closely, he was fretting over his own undesired position rather than grieving about anything else in particular.

"For this is a most awkward position," says Cesario, "into which I have been thrust by King Ferdinand—who may, after all, be my father. I had always intended to ask my mother about that, in confidence, some day after she had been drinking and was in an unusually good temper. She would probably have told me. Now my curiosity will not ever be satisfied as to a point concerning which a properly affectionate son is fairly entitled to frank information."

He scowled slightly at the still, the so aloof seeming corpse. He noted the proud lift of the chin; and it appeared to him to defy put-by life to hurt this dead woman any more. Well, but Cesario knew that in Purgatory, or in Hell even, his great-spirited if obtuse mother would endure her allotted punishments just as unconquerably.

"Meanwhile it is I who am being punished, here, by King Ferdinand, for the good of his kingdom. I do not love the King of Melphé, no matter whether he be my father or not; and yet I commend him, because in logic nobody can find fault with the old gentleman's conduct. He himself has executed the King's justice upon Sebastian, where it was not possible for him to order off to execution his own nominal child. If my mother died of it, that was not his affair."

And Cesario said also: "Gratiano's death was a great loss to the welfare of Melphé. But the manner of Gratiano's death was an especially deep hurt to the welfare of Melphé, because if only Sebastian— of all living persons—had not killed Gratiano, so very tactlessly, without any polite concealment, why then, in default of getting Poland, Sebastian could at any rate have succeeded him as Cardinal of

San Marco. It followed that the heavy-faced gray schemer had to patch up his shattered statecraft extempore; and he did this by the really brilliant stroke of killing Sebastian, with his own hand, in public. He thus satisfied justice; he silenced all possible criticism; and he nevertheless protected Melphé, by thrusting me into slain Gratiano's place. These expedients he did not plan out in advance. He must have improvised them in the self-same instant that he first saw poor Gratiano's dead body. It was not merely sound economics which the King then displayed. The King of Melphé has genius."

Afterward Cesario said: "There is not any flaw in the King's conduct; and so, in pure logic, I applaud his conduct, as befitting a conscientious and a highly gifted monarch. Yet I cannot condone the position into which his untiring vigilance has combined with his strong sense of duty to put, of all persons, me."

"The King serves his kingdom," replied the Sieur de la Forêt, who now stood upon the other side of the small low couch, looking down toward the dead Queen in reflective consideration.

"But this"—thought Cesario, for no reason at all—"this has happened to me before."

XIX

"The King serves his kingdom," the Sieur de la Forêt repeated; and it seemed strange enough to be finding him here, thus unexplainedly, in yet another bedchamber.

—Although, in point of fact, as Cesario noticed, they had now passed into a vague corridor hung with time-faded green hangings; and as the two men walked onward, the sublime scholar continued:

"His Melphé has proved to be, just as you once predicted, an exorbitant mistress. Yet the King serves Melphé, rather than your private whims, Cesario. And for that reason, so they tell me, all Melphé prospers, under his strongly centralized government, and his capable administration, and his sound fiscal laws, and his yet other common-sense doings, such as make for the advance of every sort of material prosperity. Yet you complain!"

"I complain," Cesario agreed, "because I do not care one snap of my fingers about public welfare.

I complain because, in the clear judgment of poets, the public has not the weight of a belch or of a flea's eyelash. I complain because I do not like the run of mankind; because as an artist, I despise them; and because as a rational creature, I perceive that upon no logical grounds does the public merit any welfare. I complain because persons whom I loved have been murdered. And finally, without any ill-advised grumbling, but with shrieks, I complain because, for the sake of this trivial, gimcrack, infernal public welfare, I, who am by nature a poet, have been made willy-nilly a prince of Holy Church."

The sympathetic bearing of the Sieur de la Forêt continued to be equalled only by the majesty of his demeanor. Yet he said merely:

"Your sudden scarlet outbreak into the robes of a cardinal, my prince, is but the forerunning symptom of a condition far more grave and more serious. When the present Pontiff dies of gravel, within the next month or two months, then the votes of the Sacred College which were purchased in Gratiano's support will be cast for the Cardinal of San Sixtus. He is past seventy years old. At that age, you conceive, one can die at virtually any moment without evoking harsh criticism. Well! and when Buoncompagno does die—rather speedily after his elevation to the Papacy—these same votes will go to you. As King and as Pope, the house of Vetori will then be the chief house in Christendom; and Melphé will be well served."

"But I do not wish to be Pope!" Cesario returned. "And besides, the Pope is not dying of gravel, or of any other disorder. The Holy Father as yet lives in excellent health."

"Indeed," said the Sieur de la Forêt, "the hearty appetite and the vigor and the fine digestion of Pope Pius are proverbial. Yet his cook is King Ferdinand's pensioner."

Cesario saw the point.

"So," said Cesario, "so it has been arranged, quite as if Carneschi still lived, that for the good of Melphé we are to poison two popes in succession? Well, and nobody can find fault with that forthright stroke of policy, either, just in itself. Toxicology has its acknowledged place, as a branch of statesmanship, among all diplomats. But I, you conceive, I am by nature not diplomatic. I am a poet. I have no faculty, I possess no innate talent, for killing people in this plodding and conscientious fashion. Nor do I desire to become head of the Church, and thus to incur the responsibility of being the representative of Heaven upon a planet which Heaven manages, as I cannot but remark, in a most inefficient manner."

"I sympathize with you, Cesario; and indeed I have heard of a logic-loving deity who left heaven —a long while before the Trinity that is now in power had any popes—rather than incur a responsibility so shocking and in fact outrageous."

"Aha! and what became of this ancient deity?"

"Nobody knows, my prince. It is only a legend, a bit of old wives' folk-lore. Every word of it is nonsense, no doubt. Yet this legend says that he retired into the forest of Branlon, to live as the Lord of the Forest, according to his own tastes, among his elect few followers."

Cesario asked then, "How do they live in Branlon?"

Messire de la Forêt answered this at some length; and Cesario, still walking slowly at his side, in this endless-seeming corridor, heard the improbable story with a grave and a steadily increasing attention.

"Truly, that is a better way of living," says Cesario, by-and-by, "than I am likely to find here in Melphé, now that I have been involved in the sordid routine of royal affairs. I feel that I dislike equally the vocation of a pope and of a poisoner. So I shall avoid these responsibilities; and in the strange woods of Branlon, Lord of the Forest, it may be that I also shall live in the fine manner which you have described to me with the eloquence of ten seraphim."

"Hah, but, Cesario, what about your patriotism, and your conscience, and the more noble side of your nature in general? Do not these declare to you, very sternly, that it is not proper to evade the responsibilities of your position, or for you to upset the welfare of a flesh-and-blood kingdom, through the pursuit of your personal pleasure?"

"No, Lord of the Forest, they declare to me nothing of the sort: for Melphé is Ferdinand's kingdom, as after his sedate descent into Hell, it will belong to Lorenzo. I have not any part in Melphé. Now that you have told me about your own kingdom, I know that it is not Melphé, but Branlon only, which is the native home of all poets.

The sublime scholar smiled. But he said also:

"Inasmuch as the better side of your nature remains thus regrettably taciturn, Cesario, I must

now, in common fairness, appeal to your more de-
graded instincts. I shall therefore ask what do you
intend doing about your sworn oath to be revenged
upon Hypolita?"

"I dismiss that oath," says Cesario, handsomely,
"since it was made upon only five Bibles during
what, after all, I now regard as a moment of bad
temper. The fair strumpet is married to Pescaro.
She has gone with him into his native Pania. She
may there endure whatsoever the fates may allot to
Hypolita, without any murderous intermeddling
by me."

"And what of Hermia?"

Cesario's face altered. He said, as the two men
walked always onward in the long corridor hung
with time-faded green.

"Truly, she is a grave dear child, whom I love,
somewhat. I could have been happy enough as fond
Hermia's husband. But that has become uncanon-
ical. A cardinal is denied no luxury except only a
wife. I cannot marry Hermia, now that old Ferdinand's statesmanship has thus pitchforked me into
the adhesive arms of Mother Church."

"Do you remember, though, Cesario, that he has
affairs in train to make you the head of that as yet
thriving organization. I hold no brief for Jahveh;

and in fact I have never been able to get on with the *nouveaux riches.* Yet this former storm-god of Sinai is well spoken of by many of His better paid employees. That is why, in mere fairness, I must bid you bear in mind that, simply through turning back now, you will shortly be acclaimed as the Successor of St. Peter, as Bishop of Rome, as Archbishop and Metropolitan of the Roman Province, as Primate of the West, and as supreme Pontiff of the Universal Church."

Cesario shrugged; and as they still passed onward, through the long corridor, Cesario said:

"Very truly, a pope is acclaimed handsomely in all parts of Christendom, as well as, I have no least doubt, in Paradise also. Yet to my mind, it is better to be acclaimed as a poet in the green aisles of Branlon. So let us be going to that place, Lord of the Forest."

PART THREE: THE AFFAIRS OF FERDINAND

XX

They record how King Ferdinand, after he had got to be a king through murder and thieving, ruled with mildness and thrift. In some respects his Melphé as yet left, for the more religious, a hope of still sweeter benefactions to follow by-and-by after your decease. Melphé, continued, respectfully and without undue ostentation, to fall short of Paradise. But when you compared King Ferdinand's Melphé with some more contiguous, earthly kingdom, of which the monarch desired glory and greatness, then did sedate unenterprising Melphé appear inexplicable, and its burghers blessed, and its king a contriver of quiet, small, daily miracles.

For nowadays, under King Ferdinand, flourished contentment and a well-to-do peacefulness. This king did not make war, upon any provocation; instead, he made treaties thriftily—gaining by them as the rule, and even in less happy instances losing far less than a superb victory upon the battle-field would have cost his kingdom. His people, who regarded their overlord without any enthusiasm, and who indeed made fun of a monarch so unheroic, regarded also, with a continuing wonder, their own fat prosperity. It contented them, almost, for their lack of a more ornamental ruler who would have preferred blood and trumpets and his subjects' misery.

Moreover, you found in Melphé no large injustice, barring only the King's prompt infliction of it whensoever he considered injustice expedient to the state's welfare; for upon such occasions he confiscated, or he murdered, with a large lack of compunction. But he did not do this very often, nor except of necessity. For the most part, he allowed affairs to proceed lullingly, under his unblinking inspection. There was thus no public disorder, nor was there any tiny least delay in the unsparing punishment of those who infringed against the King's rather numerous but yet lenient new laws: and probity did actually govern in every department of state, after his chief of police, and then his chamberlain, and still later, two judges of the supreme court—each one of them having been convicted of embezzlement and extortion—were deprived of office in the morning and of manhood during the afternoon. They were gelded upon an open, low platform, which had been made superbly gay in their honor, with scarlet and white hangings, under the fine palm-trees which adorned the plaza of San Marco.

Trade prospered handsomely throughout Melphé, especially in silks, and wools, and brocades. The export of tapestries had doubled; that of sulphur, tripled. Two new cathedrals were begun, one at Sinapoli, the other at Serli. Roads and good harbors and adequate sewerage had been provided everywhere. In San Marco a university was established; at Alcarses a guano factory was opened in the interest of scientific farming; all the more wholesome, second-rate forms of art were patronized with discretion; and San Marco had become the third largest jewel-market in Christendom, for, as has been reported, the King loved gems, and he purchased them liberally. It was, they said, his one weakness.

So the jewel merchants came to San Marco, bringing their bright wares to King Ferdinand. And always he haggled with them; but in the end he bought.

He bought constantly. He bought with discretion. And so, nowadays, the King had jewels without their equals. From all quarters of the world his jewels came to him.

He had pearls, from the gulf of Manaar, and from the Persian gulf, and from Borneo; and pink pearls, from the West Indies; and black pearls, from the gulf of Mexico. From Golconda and from Brazil the King got diamonds, of all sizes and of eleven colors, including the black diamond and the very rare green diamond. And besides that he got rubies, both male and female, and rubies of each caste, including the oriental ruby and the rubicelle and the spinel and the balas ruby. He got emeralds from Upper Egypt and from the Ural mountains. He got sapphires, of the admired right cornflower blue, from Rakwara; and reddish-blue sapphires, from Battambang; and yellow-tinged sapphires, from Krat; and very dark-blue sapphires, that had been fetched all the long way from Madagascar.

Nor was that above a fourth of his bright hoardings, because in three other tall cabinets made out of satin-wood the King kept stored, nowadays, much curiously carved amber dug from the graves of Iceland; and jade in the shape of fighting-cocks

and of bats and of slim, slant-eyed goddesses and
of butterflies, that had come from the musk-
scented darkness of remote Chinese tombs; and
moonstones, from out of Hindustan, which, under
penalty of an old curse, must always be kept
wrapped in yellow cloth; and lapis lazuli bracelets
that had been worn by the Syrian wife of the second Nebuchadnezzar; and chrysolites fetched, by
trained cormorants, from the Island of Serpents in
the Red Sea, that island from which no human being had ever returned alive; and five quaint necklaces made of rock crystal and of sard and of onyx,
diversified with pendants of carnelian, that had
been found in the mummy case of a Pharaoh of the
Middle Empire called Antef; and two large heavy
brooches of gold filigree, inset with garnets and
meerschaum, which had been taken from the long
barrow of a Viking pirate named Amleth, who had
once ruled over Jutland. There was, in brief, not
any sort of jewel, from any coign of earth, which
King Ferdinand did not purchase, and then hide
away, like a sedate magpie, in one or the other of
his four satin-wood cabinets.

All these things do the historians of Melphé
record.

XXI

The historians of Melphé record likewise how King Ferdinand talked with Hermia, saying,—

"Madonna, it is you, if anyone, who must know what has become of my son, the departed Cardinal Cesario."

She replied: "But, majesty, I do not know. I know only that it is reported he went into the woods of Branlon with a most notable scholar who is called the Sieur de la Forêt."

"Yet the boy loved you," says the King. "He gave me no peace until I had consented to his marrying you. As cardinal, he could not marry you, to be sure. But you could have lived in all honor and comfort as his mistress. For these reasons, it is not plausible that Cesario should have run away into Branlon with a garrulous tall scholar clothed in fern-colored green."

"Majesty, I did not say anything about the Sieur de la Forêt's clothing, or his talkativeness either."

"That was not needed, madonna. I have my police. Besides, you become discursive. The true point is that Cesario would not ever have run away with anybody, whether in green or in scarlet or in salmon-pink, without any word to you whom he so much loved."

"It was not I, sir, whom he loved, but my sister."

"Yet it was to you—or so, in any event, I had understood—that he was betrothed. You, at any rate, wear a particularly fine ring which the boy stole from me."

If the King had hoped to startle her, he was disappointed. Hermia said, with entire calmness,—

"That is so, majesty."

"And how did this come about?"

"I would prefer not to tell you."

The King looked at this small, quiet Greek lady for some while. He said, temperately:

"In this world, madonna, we do not all always get our preferences, not even by being stubborn with the overlords of this world. I am one of them. And my curiosity is considerable."

She replied, "Nobody doubts that, majesty; for we know what means you employ, in your torture chambers, to satisfy this same curiosity."

"You do not know one half the truth as to my torture chambers," then said King Ferdinand—"as yet."

"And do you threaten me, sir, with an increase of knowledge?"

"I would but exhort you, small spitfire, to an increase of civility—yes, and of consideration too. I would ask you to remember that, as you yourself are now proving, in dealing with a king no one of his subjects is frank. Whose fault is it, then, if a king employs persuaders to induce candor with such instruments as may be necessary?"

Hermia did not answer. That she considered the gray tyrant of Melphé to be talking nonsense, she did not hide at all.

So the rebuffed King said, by-and-by: "Nevertheless, small spitfire, I do not design, not just at present, to interrogate you either upon the rack or with thumbscrews. It is merely that I do not understand the heart-affairs in which you are somehow involved. Cesario had my consent to marry your father's daughter. And of his own choice, so you tell me, he chose the daughter whom he did not prefer. I begin, should you permit the observation, to think that he acted with uncharacteristic good sense. Yet I do not at all understand what kind of miracle could have betrayed Cesario into displaying any good sense."

Then Hermia said an odd thing, a thing utterly lacking in decorum.

"You are a strange old gentleman, majesty," she remarked, gravely. "You browbeat people. You torture people. And yet at bottom you are kind-hearted. I think too you are lonely."

"Madonna," he replied, "you have laid bare, at one glance, the two secrets which I had hidden from everybody else."

She looked at him, reflectively, for some while. She was judging him; and the verdict was favorable.

Afterward, speaking very quietly, Hermia told the King the exact truth, so far as she knew it, as to what had happened upon Gratignolles. The King listened with grim scowling attention to this matter-of-fact and unemotional young woman.

She ended her story; and then the King sighed, without any sign of grief, but in mild dissatisfaction, saying:

"You have been badly used, child, through my need to serve Melphé. That is unfortunate. You might have made out of Cesario something cloudily resembling a man. In the outcome it may be that he is lost to both of us, because they who go into

Branlon do not return of their own accord. We must see about that. I still have need of him. Meanwhile, I have need of you also."

"And in what way, majesty?"

The King answered, scowling yet more ferociously: "Since the death of my late Queen, small spitfire, I have been pestered beyond endurance by the ladies of my court. They consider it unbecoming, and a threat to the old morals of Melphé, that the King of Melphé should be maintaining not even one mistress. I have no special need of a mistress. Yet my people expect it of me that I should live in some such childlike iniquity; and one must honor the proprieties. Now your ways suit me. So it is you who shall be my mistress from this day forward."

"No," said Hermia.

"Oh, very well," said the King, "then, since you are pig-headed, I will marry you—but only morganatically. You cannot be my Queen, because some day some alliance or another may raise the need for me to marry a princess. Yet I will make you my morganatic wife, because I at all events have not any of your womanlike obstinacy, praise Heaven!"

[132]

"But I do not love you, sir."

"Fiddle-faddle!" said the King. "Why should you? I do not inspire love but fear. That is why you are trembling at this very instant."

"But I am not trembling, sir."

"No; but you ought to be. So the principle stays the same."

"Majesty," Hermia replied, in mild desperation, "that does not mean anything."

"On the contrary, it means that I quite understand you are in love with Cesario. Yet you cannot marry Cesario, for three excellent reasons. He has vanished; he is not in love with you; and he is a cardinal. Me you can marry; and to be the wife of a king is better, alike from all worldly and all moral standpoints, than to be the strumpet of a clergyman. Do you deny these plain truisms?"

"I deny nothing, sir. Why on earth should I deny it, when I am not arguing about any such nonsense, one way or the other?"

"Do not try to confuse the issue by asking me irrelevant questions," the King returned, sternly. "It is your duty, as my humble subject, and as a person who is suitably abashed by the force of my brilliant arguments, to answer questions, and not to ask them."

"What questions, sir?"

"It appears to me," then says King Ferdinand, "that, in addition to having stolen my bezoar ring, and in defiance of my direct orders, you are now asking me yet another question. Such conduct is called lèse majesté; and the appointed punishment is, I believe, somewhat severe."

"Still, sir—"

King Ferdinand banged down his fist upon the oak desk beside him.

"Young woman, and will you not ever stop arguing with me?"

"But, sir, I am not arguing—"

"Your statement, madonna, is self-contradictory—unless it indeed signifies that you are now calling your sovereign a liar to his face. What do you mean by these outrages? Why can you not be more sensible?"

"Yet it appears to me, majesty, that it is you—"

"To complete your statement," the King warned her, "would be high treason. You balk at no crime, it seems; and I am really at a loss whether to wonder the more at your shameless iniquity or your high-handed foolishness. However, you have at least stolen one of my most valuable rings. That special offence, alone in the long catalogue of your enormities, seems encouraging. Do you love jewels?" he shot at her.

"I think that all women love jewels, majesty."

"Very well, then," said the King—unlocking the tall satin-wood cabinet to the left side of him, and taking out from it, at random, a resplendent handful of brooches and rings, and a coronet, and four bracelets, and two of old Antef's necklaces,—"then, through mere pity, I shall have to bribe you into behaving with a somewhat less criminal insanity, by giving you such jewels as no other woman possesses. Impudence and sheer feeble-mindedness can get a large dividend out of this world, I would have you note, when they ask for it with a young girl's lips. So do you take your pick of these now, as a betrothal gift; and when you have married me, you can have them all."

"They are marvelous. They rather frighten me," said small Hermia, in a small voice. "And I could never resist emeralds. It is only—"

The King snarled.

"It is only because your strutting Cesario is

[135]

young, and handsome, and can make phrases for you. It is only because you do not like me, because I am ugly to look at, and because I am quite old enough to know better than to be bothering myself about any woman breathing." Then the King grumbled,—

"Nevertheless, you do bother me; and so I intend to marry you."

Leaning forward, with an habitual friendly gesture, Hermia stroked the back of his square-shaped, brown-spotted hand, very lightly, two or three times.

"Please do not be foolish," she begged of him. "But, majesty, I do like you, a great deal. So far as that goes, I like you better than I like Cesario, because you are kind-hearted and very lonely and strong. Now Cesario is not any one of these things."

"No," said the King, "Cesario, if indeed he still lives, is a mere minor poet. There is no pith to him."

"But your hand trembles, majesty."

"That is because you are touching it, my dear. So the affair is settled."

Small Hermia considered the King gravely. She did not follow his deduction; she most certainly did not grant it: but she did feel, without any special sense of surprise, that she quite honestly liked the ageing tyrant of Melphé. In fact, she pitied him, for some reason or another, she did not know why.

Then it occurred to her that, with a woman to look after him, the second button would not have been missing from his doublet. The entire room, and even the top of the King's desk, needed dusting, as she now noticed; for that of course was just how your servants did treat you when you were only a kind-hearted lonely old gentleman who pretended to browbeat people. And for the rest, the all-powerful King had trembled when but a moment ago, in a light gust of compassion, she had touched him, merely as she would have touched her father or any other familiar acquaintance, without really thinking about the matter one way or the other.

The girl deduced, with entire correctness, that King Ferdinand did not have anywhere in this world any familiar acquaintance. The poor gruff, gray, lonely, rather dear old blusterer had only a parcel of good-for-nothing servants, who neglected him, quite shamefully, even down to his gold buttons.

Hermia said, by-and-by: "The King honors me. Let us send for my father."

XXII

All, after that, was quickly arranged. To begin
with, the King ordered,—

"Fetch in my tailor."

To the tailor, he says: "Adorni, I am being married this evening. I shall need some new clothes."

"But, majesty, there is not time—"

"There had better be time," said the King, "if
you indeed wish to sit down to supper in flesh and
blood." Then Ferdinand added:

"Decorum demands a sort of half mourning. Let
us say purple, with as much gold trimming as seems
suitably optimistic. Now go away. Tell them to
send in the Druids of Rorn."

XXIII

In came these celebrated and all-cultured and
omniscient persons, one following the other, as was
their unfailing custom. They lined up before Ferdinand as if for a review. There were four of them,
because they came from all quarters; and of them
the King demanded,—

"What has your supreme wisdom revealed to you concerning the forest of Branlon?"

They answered him, saying severally:

"Branlon is a decadent nostalgia."

"Branlon is pastiche."

"Branlon is old hat."

"Branlon is sophomoric."

The King said: "Stop talking! And then tell me where is this so various Branlon."

"Majesty," replied one druid, "you mistake. Branlon is not a bit various."

Then another druid explained, "No; for the absurd, lewd ways of Branlon are repetitious, as, for goodness only knows how long, we have all been saying, over and yet over again, because we abhor repetition."

But the third druid declared, "Branlon is pseudo this, and pseudo that, and"—he half whispered it, with a flustered blushing—"quite possibly pseudo the other."

"In brief," said the fourth druid, "Branlon is a place so negligible that we have emitted thousands upon thousands of words to make clear the fact that no intelligent person takes any notice of Branlon."

"Stop talking!" says King Ferdinand. "The affair is that my son Cesario has gone into Branlon. And I desire to know what power will release him."

They answered:

"Time, it may be."

"—Or piety, perhaps."

"—Or, just possibly, an honest innate taste for dulness."

"—Because all these three," explained the fourth druid, "are strong enemies to the Lord of the Forest and his thin tinselled magic."

"Very well, then!" says King Ferdinand. "Stop talking! And do you now employ your time and your piety and your innate taste for dulness, each in the proper manner, until, through these most respectable agencies, my son Cesario shall have been evicted from Branlon."

They replied to him, all speaking in unison: "Majesty, we will indeed do what we may to preserve your unfortunate son. For the forest which now imprisons him is a world of half-lights and of strange melancholy repose. Its vague sunlight falls, with a diluted radiancy, through quite impossibly shaped clouds, upon purple uplands which are not properly cultivated by up-to-date farmers; its moonshine illumines glades where no timber merchant has as yet established his sawmill. Magic flourishes in these glades with a regrettable profusion. Your son has entered into a place made wonderful with secresy, a place of which every beauty is ambiguous, a place of pale languid sorceries. He consorts with centaurs and with dryads also. His companions are not endorsed by zoölogy. Irresponsible uncharted caverns have opened before him, revealing their stores of frail fairy gold. He has been made free of castles that glow with an inward radiancy not ever boasted by any other castle save only the gleaming home of fair-haired Menelaus, wherein dwelt Helen."

And they said moreover: "Majesty, we will indeed do what we may to preserve your unfortunate son. In the forest which imprisons him, the streams glitter, but they murmur wistfully, and it is as if their quiet rippling whispered to him about some happiness long overpast beyond human recovery. The birds of this forest sing wistfully, without any full-throated gladness. Its dragons ramp with undue urbanity; they intimidate nobody. And always, somewhere, not very far away, sounds the wistful, the breathless, the half-sorrowful mirth of women who display proclivities which we, as earnest-minded persons, cannot but deplore. Everywhere your departed Cesario encounters women who are well shaped and well colored and undisfigured by intellectual excesses. He meets fine lovely women, enamoured women, frank women, complaisant women, recurring everywhere, in his sylvan paradise, with the monotonous regularity of a pattern in a wallpaper. Mohammed was not able to invent a paradise any better calculated to overcrowd hell with earnest-minded persons. And besides that, in his troubled hearing rings the echoing of such sardonic yapped-out laughter as a potbellied satyr might give vent to, did he suddenly find himself conscience-ridden and a prey to chivalrous sentiments."

Then they said: "Majesty, we will indeed do what we may to preserve your unfortunate son. For his prison is builded out of pastiche and decadent nostalgia; he stays ensorcelled in a sophomoric old hat. He does not hearken, as all we hearken, very earnest-mindedly, to the noise of hammers and of saws and of blatant persons speaking constructively. He is not suitably excited about an industrial revolution. Through some grave moral malady, he does not think at every instant about class struggles. He prefers to be hearing, in his unmagnanimous unconcern as to the proletariat, an elfin music. Yet always sorrow cries out to your misguided son, cries skirlingly, among the sweet and thin cadences of this ancient music; for through the purple shadows, and between the long, thin golden fingers of sunset, grin at him death's white teeth; and he notes death, strong death, held back from him by thin glittering colors and by thin radiant mists, held back from him by a thin leash of filigree, and for how brief a while!"

The King grunted.

"Do what you can for him," says King Ferdinand, "if there indeed be any such absurd forest: and stop talking! Ask how my tailor is getting on. Tell them to send in Lord Lysander of Gratignolles."

XXIV

"Sit down," the King resumed, addressing Lysander, "and then get up, because you are leaving my court at once. I am granting you forty acres in the parish of San Piero, a farm and buildings near

Spreto, a very fertile estate at Neri which formerly belonged to Giulio Grimoard, and a monopoly of the supply of seines, of shrimp, and of all seafish, excepting only oysters, to the city of Bescaglia. This monopoly is at present a crown grant to Guido dei Castelli so long as he lives, but that will be arranged. He has been embezzling from the town treasury."

"But, majesty—" said Lysander, in a mere whirl.

"I am giving you this property," the King went on, "because I intend to make of your daughter my morganatic wife. I believe her name is Hermia. I am sending you away because your position here would be awkward. A morganatic wife is neither fish, flesh, nor poultry. Moreover, you might be trying to influence her, and through her, me. I do not desire to be influenced. My nature is far too plastic. You have, therefore, an hour in which to say good-bye to your daughter. And her name, by the way,—her name is Hermia, is it not?"

Lysander, gulping and a-tremble with joy, replied only:

"She is called Hermia. She is a good girl, majesty.

Without her, my life will be wholly empty. Yet with such wealth I can buy many books."

Thereupon the flustered, time-ruined poet went back to his island home, and to the dustiness of his library. And the King ordered,—

"Send in Sacrobosco."

XXV

To Sacrobosco, the King says: "Messer Guido dei Castelli, the syndic, is about to exchange his present shifty way of living for that life which is eternal. He will do this the first moment that you can waylay him without creating any public disturbance. The police have been told about it. They will not interfere. I do not imagine my reasons for expediting the King's justice, thus informally, would be to you of any special interest; and inasmuch as I am being married this evening, I have not the time to explain my reasons."

His favorite assassin answered, all one huge, bearded, scarlet, shrugging protest:

"You speak, sir, as if my faith in your judgment were not implicit. The truth is quite otherwise. I desire only to offer my respectful congratulations.

One does not, in this imperfect world, get married every day." Then Sacrobosco asked,—

"Yet need it be to-night?"

"And why, pray, Sacrobosco, should I not be married to-night? And what have you to do with it?"

"Majesty, far be it from the thoughts of Sacrobosco to interfere with any matter so important! I refer merely to the murder. And I would not inquire, you conceive, did it not happen to be my son's sixth birthday. Already his cake has been prepared, and his small playmates are gathering in our home for their innocent mirth—"

The King grumbled. "Never, you tall hairy rascal, can I get service from you when I ask for it. Always you have one excuse or another; you become inefficient; and your patients end by dying of old age."

"Ah, but, majesty," Sacrobosco pleaded, "but we are to play at blindman's buff! I had promised him that. And it is so very difficult to explain, to a child of six, the more beneficial aspects of my profession. In infancy one does not comprehend these economic needs. There is even a prejudice."

[146]

—To which the King replied fretfully. He replied, with an undisguised and enraged scowl:

"Very well, then. Here, Sacrobosco, do you buy for your infernal brat something with this—but not anything useful. Instead, do you let him pick out for himself something with which he can make unpleasant noises, or induce indigestion, or otherwise enjoy himself, with the King's compliments. Any time before Thursday will serve quite as well for Castelli's throat-cutting. So do you see to it. Ask how the tailor is getting on. And tell them to send in the ambassador from Bracciano."

XXVI

Then with Guy of Glasignac the King haggled, for some twenty minutes, over the proposed new naval treaty. The terms of it suited both of them well enough, but each hoped to gain a little more,— King Ferdinand through delay, and Glasignac through the death of King Ferdinand, for which Glasignac had arranged. So they by-and-by left the treaty unconcluded, each having declared any such unfair terms to be out of the question; and Glasignac was about to withdraw, invoking the zenith as to King Ferdinand's lack of mere common reason, when the elder man remarked,—

"We have caught Grimoard, by the way."

"And who, majesty, may be this Grimoard?" asked Glasignac, in bland innocence.

"I will show you," replied Ferdinand, amiably; and he then led Glasignac into the King's torture chamber, where three skilled persons had temporarily put by their work upon Grimoard, and a clerk was writing down the half-dead man's confession, thus far.

"If only he had not sneezed," the King continued, with sympathy, "then, no doubt, he would have succeeded in killing me. But those worthless servants of mine do not ever sweep up my rooms properly. So the unfortunate creature was found under my bed, the night before last, with his long sword and his two daggers and his three letters from your master, my good son-in-law, each signed in full Paolo Giordano d'Orsini."

"They were all forgeries, beyond doubt," remarked Glasignac.

"By the very best of luck, they were transparent forgeries," the King agreed, gravely, "for otherwise, I would now have to go to war with my son-in-law. Yes; they were all forgeries. Still, Glasignac, it might be as well for you to remind Paolo of two plain truisms: the first being that no sane person would ever put down any such highly dangerous matter in writing; and the second, that my impatient good son-in-law shall not ever inherit Melphé, not even through stabbing me in my sleep."

"Majesty," returned Glasignac, with a respectful candor—after he had made sure, unostentatiously, that the assassin whom he had hired to kill Ferdinand was now, through good luck, unconscious,—"majesty, we all pray that you may live forever; and that your son Prince Lorenzo may yet beget many sons and daughters. But, failing any favorable response to our daily prayers, and now that your other sons are all dead, my master is indeed the next heir, by right of his wife, your sole surviving daughter."

—To which the King replied only: "My friend, I created the kingdom of Melphé. And I have decided that my life's work shall not ever become tributary to Bracciano and Anguillaria. This much I may now tell you, with that noble frankness which is one of my most lovable traits."

Then, turning toward where Grimoard lay unconscious but still feebly moaning upon the rack, gray Ferdinand thumped the bared chest of Grimoard.

"A fine stout fellow!" the King said, admiringly. "In fact, I have never seen such a growth of hair: it would do credit to the chest of a bull. If only he had kept out of politics, this superb young man might have lived to be a hundred. Meanwhile it is in every way a compliment that so much brawn and muscle should have been thought necessary to dispose of me. I appreciate it, Glasignac. What has he confessed to since I was here this morning?" King Ferdinand then inquired of the clerk; and the King forthwith began reading.

It was a rather lengthy report, over which the King scowled.

"This is better," he said, "but it is not the complete truth. Still, it incriminates Della Rovere. Now, but however in this world, Glasignac, did you persuade him to take part in the affair?"

"I, majesty!" says Glasignac, all horror at the mere notion.

"Ah, yes! but indeed, my friend, I had forgotten your complete innocence. Do you pardon me. Well, but it is not pleasant here. So let us get back to my closet. Continue the torture, of course," Ferdinand added, as he went, with short trotting steps, out of the room; and afterward, seated again at his oak desk, after an amicable parting with Glasignac, the King looked yet once more at the clock.

"Have Della Rovere arrested," Ferdinand then ordered. "No, I meant Andrea della Rovere. I have no doubt that Alessandro, too, is involved, but against him I have not any proof as yet. So do you advise Messer Alessandro della Rovere, with the King's compliments, that if his conscience at all troubles him about anything, he would do well to leave Melphé at once. Let Andrea be put to the question, the first thing in the morning, after my poor tired tormentors have had a good night's rest. They looked like mere ghosts. Send them three bottles of Burgundy. Tell them to employ only the strappado alternated with the boot, for the first two hours, when they begin on Andrea. And let them finish with Grimoard after dinner. Ask how the tailor is getting on. Fetch in my barber. Have my chaplain in readiness. And tell everybody else to go home, for I am being married this evening, and have not any more time for them."

Thus ended the King's work for that afternoon.

XXVII

Thus, too, did it come about that King Ferdinand and Hermia were married morganatically, just before supper, by the King's chaplain. Without the blessing of Holy Church, as the King observed gravely, they could not hope to sleep well. Immediately after supper—accompanied only by ten lackeys, by three ladies in waiting, and the barber—the King and his extra-legal bride removed to the King's seaside villa near Sinapoli.

Everywhere the old gentleman's conversion from an unkinglike continence was applauded. As when the enamoured cat seeks the tiles caterwauling, then the glad rats rejoice over love's customary unvigilance, even so did the barons of Melphé pluck up heart, because, under a king engrossed by the pleasures of an avocation which they named frankly, one might hope yet again to rob and to pillage the fat burghers, in yesterday's good old fashion, without being meddled with. Even those court ladies who had in vain attempted to beguile the King into ruining their virtue could reflect that at least he had made a beginning in errancy; and that he who takes one mistress is fairly certain to take another. The poets wrote verses as to this marriage, in a vein largely indelicate. Nor did the lower classes omit to illustrate this marriage, with chalk drawings of a jocular but exaggerative nature, upon the gateways and the alley walls of San Marco.

It was, in brief, a marriage in the eyes of the church—but so far as went the law, no marriage at all—which, everybody in Melphé applauded except the one person who might lose by it. He, of course, was Prince Lorenzo.

XXVIII

It followed that, in Ferrata, Prince Lorenzo frowned at a half-emptied wine bottle, consideringly. As the late Queen of Melphé's sole surviving son—or in any event, as her only perceptible son, now that Cesario had disappeared,—plump good-natured Lorenzo knew that all his future might hinge on the nature of this Greek girl who of a sudden had become the King's wife, or the King's mistress, just as you chose to interpret matters. Either way, as Lorenzo now comprehended, with the futile rage of a congenitally lazy person who has been forced to take instant action, he would have to do something about it. Either way, this Hermia would demand watching.

"In brief," says Lorenzo, "I must felicitate my dear father upon his new-found happiness in his second marriage."

"Do you not talk to me," his wife replied, "in the same breath about marriage and happiness."

"I quite agree with you, Giovanna, that the notion is preposterous. We have well proved that, the more thanks to your selfish sterility. Still, one must be polite."

"Since when, Lorenzo, did you begin the practice of politeness? and wherever do you practise it? for most certainly it is not in this house, where I can never get a civil word out of you from one day's end to another day's end, but only this not ever ending, disgusting talk about my having a baby, at once, within the next twenty minutes."

"It would be awkward for us," Lorenzo continued, "if this girl were to bear a son, either with or without my beloved father's connivance—as she quite probably will, my dear, for you know what these Greeks are,—because in that event, the browbeating old fiend would at once be proclaiming the brat as the next heir after me. I really do not understand why you do not have any children, Giovanna," Lorenzo added, reverting to a familiar grievance. "It is not considerate of you, my dear, for now that Cesario has gone away, there is nobody to succeed me."

"And can I help that, you half-man?"

"You wrong me," Lorenzo replied, with a display of some conscious virtue, "as I could well prove by the testimony of dozens upon dozens of gentlewomen whose honesty is above suspicion. Besides, that is not the point. A more patriotic woman, in your highly responsible position, would contrive to have a few children anyhow, without of necessity dragging me into the matter."

"Now, but indeed, Lorenzo," the Princess admitted, "you are quite enough to drive any woman into adultery and into murder also! But I have my immortal soul to save."

"Do you save it, by all means. I would only counsel you to save Melphé first. Why, but you could do that in twenty minutes, Giovanna, with some clever, clean young fellow; you would probably enjoy it; and afterward you can always repent and be absolved."

—To which the Princess Giovanna returned only,—

"You ought to be ashamed of yourself!"

"Why?" says Lorenzo, somewhat astonished.

"Ask your conscience," she exhorted him, "because holy matters ought to come first. And after that, do you ask your doctor."

"Really, my dearest," remarked Lorenzo, as he went out of the room, and slammed the door behind him, "you are beyond any endurance."

After thus taking leave of his vexatiously barren and forever fault-finding wife, Lorenzo rode with but two attendants toward San Marco, to be greeted in that city with news yet more astounding than had been the news of the King's marriage. King Ferdinand, as the Prince here discovered, had resigned to Lorenzo an equal share in the government of Melphé, creating him Prince Regent.

XXIX

Now in Pania, at the selfsame instant that the Princess Giovanna rebuked Prince Lorenzo, Hypolita was saying to her own husband:

"So that minx has a king! And I have you!"

"My adored one—" replied the ever-smiling, lean Count of Pescaro, who remained frankly uxorious even after a not inconsiderable period of marriage.

"Yet which one of us is the better looking?" Hypolita demanded.

He said, "My darling—"

"Damn her!" says Hypolita.

"By all means, my pet. It is merely—"

"Meanwhile," Hypolita continued, speaking with an increased liveliness—"meanwhile, how many thousand times do I have to tell you that we ought to present our congratulations to the sly strumpet at once? Her good will is essential, you fool. If we can only keep on her soft side, then our fortunes are made."

"Yes; but—" says Pescaro.

"For the King ages," says Hypolita. "He becomes senile, that is evident. Who else but a half-blind old idiot would have picked out my dear poor Hermia? She has not even a complexion. So I shall manage her, and she him, if I can but get to San Marco."

"Why, then—" says Pescaro.

"But how can I?" Hypolita demanded—"how,

in God's name, can I ever get anywhere, Marcello?
—when you elect to sit here talking, and talking,
and talking forever, while time flies! My dear sister
does not know how to manage a man. She never
did know. And her legs are most disappointing,
they are heron's legs. Her breasts are mere nothing.
Old men like something more exuberant; they prefer to rest in comfort. So perhaps I can get the King
away from her, now he has turned lecherous. I
can then put the slut in a convent."

"Yet—" says Pescaro.

"Otherwise," says Hypolita, "I must protect the
dear child's interests, of course. She may lose the
gray fool now at any moment, without my loving
counsels to guide her. So do you stop talking, Marcello, stop talking! and have horses saddled."

At that, Pescaro, after shrugging philosophi-
cally, struck his wife to the floor. He then clutched
her most lovely throat so tightly as to prevent any
further discourse.

"My dearest," said Pescaro, tenderly, "the pair
of quite so-so horses which I borrowed from Vivaldi have been ready for the last quarter of an
hour. I too can recognize the brave knock of oppor-
tunity, my heart's sole queen. The deuce of it is,

that, to travel, one needs money. So do you get up, my beloved; and do you tell me just how much you got out of Vivaldi last night."

"Why, my dear, jealous, brutal husband," she replied, fondly kissing him, "he gave me this bracelet, in the morning, just before leaving; and it is rather handsome."

Pescaro inspected the trinket with the cool glance of an expert; and he then remarked:

"So you would barter my honor for mere sapphires! Still, as you say, they are fine stones. They will well pay our traveling expenses, I believe, without any present need for you to earn more. I am now off to the pawnbroker's, my pet. I return within two minutes. And do you have on your riding-habit within those two minutes, or else I shall quite finish choking you, my dove."

With that settled, he departed; and upon the whole, drove a good bargain with the pawnbroker.

Then the Count and his wife rode amicably toward Melphé, entering into the cathedral city of San Marco. Here they learned how the King had removed to Sinapoli, leaving vacant the Governor's Palace, and they heard also of how King Ferdinand had ceded one half his power to Prince Lorenzo. The town talked about nothing else.

They passed on, turning southerly, toward the seacoast and Sinapoli, where they crossed the Bridge of Lions. In this way did they reach the gates of the King's villa just as Lorenzo rode up.

XXX

The Prince frowned upon the Count, whom the Prince appreciated more exactly than Pescaro would have preferred. The Prince said:

"Pescaro, they had told me truly, I perceive, that the King has taken your Greek sister-in-law into his peculiar and intimate favor. And so you come here to merchandize in her dishonor."

"Highness," replied Pescaro, with a great deal of gesture, "I would distinguish. Fornication, for mere pleasure's sake, is no doubt a sin. Hah, but what of loyalty? what of religion? what, to be brief with you, of a king's spoken wish? No, highness; you mistake the issue. All we who are sound Christians do most plainly owe it to Divine Providence to obey instantly those princes whom Divine Providence, out of Its infinite wisdom, has seen fit to

[160]

raise over us. And my sweet sister-in-law, I trust, is no infidel. I would dislike to think that of her."

"You whine," says the Prince, critically.

"I applaud her piety," says Pescaro.

"Well, then, sound Christian, when I myself have come to be King of Melphé, I may find your logic acceptable. So long as I remain merely the Prince Regent, your logic halts. That does not matter. Your hypocrisies seem less important than is my strong need to make sure that no injurious woman has got into her clutches"—here the Prince coughed—"my beloved father. I am frankly worried about my beloved father. To my finding, his wits fail, because otherwise he would not ever have gone astray with this wicked creature, nor for that matter, would he have named me Regent of Melphé. Such doings are not at all like him."

Hypolita put by her riding-hood, and she spoke, sadly, but very sweetly.

"Hermia is not wicked at heart, my prince. She is only a most foolish spendthrift."

Lorenzo glanced at the intermeddling woman with impatience. Then he stared hard; and his voice shook somewhat, in the while he was saying,—

"Most beautiful, you speak riddles."

"I speak plain honesty, sir," she assured him. "In the ears of a prince it may ring harshly. I cannot help that. My chastity, more dear to me than is my life, more dear than is even my beloved husband, assures me that any woman is a spendthrift who parts with the most precious jewel of her honor. For she loses that which cannot ever be restored. She courts moral bankruptcy. And it is for this reason that I had ridden hither to implore my misguided sister to forsake her present infamous way of living."

"Come now, my pet! and do you be gracious, my prince," says Pescaro, who was all at sea in this welter of lofty declarings. "You must pardon my wife's rustic sentiments."

"To the contrary," replied Lorenzo, who was still looking at Hypolita with bright languishing eyes, "I am much interested by your wife's sentiments. I desire that she should explain them to me at more ample leisure."

"Eh!" says Pescaro; and he now regarded the Prince with the cool glance of an expert.

"—In private," Lorenzo continued.

"Aha!" says the Count, rubbing his hands together.

"—And for choice, in bed, Pescaro."

"Why, but indeed, highness," says the beaming Count, "you are in the right, as always. For there is no place more conducive to leisure, and no place more private, than is a bed."

"I had not known," Lorenzo continued, ignoring him, "that so much of beauty could be united with so much of goodness and of wisdom also. Your sentiments have delighted my judgment, lady, in the same instant that the charms of your person have taken my heart."

"What little beauty I may have, sir," Hypolita answered, with gentle dignity, "I must now regard as an evil, since it has led you thus to insult me."

"Hah, madonna," Lorenzo exclaimed, in surprise, "but how may the devoted true love of a prince be thought about as an insult?"

"Very truly, sir, I had forgotten that you are a prince. To me your exalted rank does not matter, but only your great wickedness—a wickedness which appears doubly shocking in a person so graceful and accomplished."

Well, and at that, Lorenzo smirked.

"—For it is not right of you, my prince," Pescaro's aggrieved wife continued, "to be speaking about love to an honorable chaste married woman; and it is not right of me, either, to have been thinking about how very handsome you were, even in the moment that you were insulting me. For you would tempt me to commit adultery. Oh, but that is most wicked of you, sir, inasmuch as adultery is a great sin. Indeed, as I must make bold to remind you, my dear prince, there is an explicit Divine commandment against adultery."

"Aha! and so you have learning likewise!" cried out Lorenzo, in large admiration. "You are acquainted with the Decalogue. That is a strange coincidence, for I too have read it. It is a most interesting piece of literature, composed by an Author Who, even though He be no longer in fashion, was yet, for His time and His barbarous surroundings, blessed with considerable talents. So we must talk about the Decalogue yet further, my dear, at complete leisure, and in private, somewhere. Pescaro,"—the Prince added—"your wife is a paragon. I am charmed with her. Do you bring her to my rooms to-night, at about eight o'clock, in order that we may continue our discussion of the Decalogue."

"But I will not come tamely to my dishonor,"

replied Hypolita, "at eight o'clock. No, nor at nine o'clock either. Let us be leaving this wicked place, Marcello, for I dare not stay here where my dear lost sister has fallen into gross sin and my own chastity is threatened."

With that, Hypolita rode off, in a superb glow of moral indignation; and she was followed by her perturbed husband.

XXXI

"Soul of my life," says Pescaro, "you are triply a fool. Sane persons do not talk such balderdash. One does not flout in this way the affections of a prince of the blood. And besides that, it was our errand to curry favor with your as yet unseen sister, inside that red-roofed villa from which we are now riding away."

"No, Marcello," Hypolita replied, kindly enough, "I am not a fool."

"Then why, my pet, do you enact one? I am not prudish; but I blushed just now to hear your nonsense."

She said, with remorse: "I admit it was too stiff. It lacked the smooth right flavor of oiliness. I

become rusty in the exercise of the more mag-
niloquent virtues since you and I began to share
the same mattress, Marcello, now and then."

"Why, but"—Pescaro pointed out—"one must
live."

"One must, my dear."

Pescaro's adoring wife regarded him pensively;
and her smiling was more sad than usual.

"Even two must live," she continued, "if it can
be managed with comfort. So you and I do live,
as yet, in fair comfort, do we not, Marcello?"

"Delight of my existence, you underestimate
matters," he protested, courteously. "For all that
we have been married so long, we are still like fond
turtle-doves when you lack clients."

"Yes, my beloved Marcello: for our deep devotion to each other, irrespective of mere bodily happenings, retains its fine and pure-hearted romance
unabated. Meanwhile, as I was about to observe, one
sees at a glance that my next seducer has an easy-
going and generous nature."

"He would pay us immeasurably better than did
Vivaldi," Pescaro agreed.

"Moreover," said Hypolita, "he is far handsomer.

He has the good looks of Cesario, without any of Cesario's annoying intelligence."

"Then why, in high Heaven's name, my adored wife, did you not encourage the fat fool in his lecherousness?"

Hypolita answered this as if half absent-mindedly. She was regarding the future; and that which her large violet-colored eyes perceived there, constrained them to look upon Pescaro with a sort of indulgent pity.

"My dear husband, but you are indeed short-sighted. To a mere prince I might have succumbed profitably—"

"And that, my pet, seems to me the precise point."

"—But how far more, my love," she continued, thoughtfully, "it will mean for your ever-faithful wife to defy the evil designs of the Prince Regent! of one who is virtually a king already, and who to-morrow will be a king duly crowned! This chub, this fat golden carp, needs playing, I can assure you, quite as if he were a fine strong salmon. So it is best for me to be virtuous, just now, at the very top of my voice. And as a virtuous woman, I must of course decline to associate with any person in my sister's compromising condition. Yes, my poor Marcello; for I intend henceforward to be more than a mere meek hanger-on to old Ferdinand's dull-witted pigmy trollop."

"Eh, my dearest"—the Count asked dubiously—"but how much more?"

"We shall see."

And Hypolita still spoke rather moodily, because the notion of Pescaro's not impossible doom as yet appeared to her kindly nature abhorrent. All that, however, could wait. She dismissed the harrowing thought of it. She said only,—

"I esteem it meanwhile my duty to confess to you, my love, that I somewhat ardently prefer the Prince to Vivaldi, or to Salviati, or to Colonna, or in fact to any other one of your recent vicars."

Pescaro laughed at that; and declared:

"For you to think well of this fat-faced man is excellent, so far as it goes. It would indeed lend zest to your evenings if all sped well. The great trouble is that, as I can but repeat, you have repulsed the Prince Regent. You have galloped away from him talking such insane balderdash as would deject Priapus. So what follows next, heart's darling?"

"Why, unless I be sadly mistaken," Hypolita returned, with that serenity of conscience which only a perfect complexion can ever give to a Christian gentlewoman, "the Prince follows."

XXXII

Nevertheless, the Prince Regent did not follow, if only because, at this instant, he had in charge matters more imperative, now that King Ferdinand had astounded everybody by handing over to Lorenzo all Melphé. To speak with precision, the rulership of this kingdom was henceforward divided. The King retained his management of foreign affairs; but after supervising in person the transfer, to his villa at Sinapoli, of his four cabinets of jewels, his favorite pair of slippers, and his furred green dressing gown, he had relinquished to Lorenzo the Governor's Palace in San Marco as well as complete control over the internal government of Melphé.

"Now that I have you, small spitfire," the King had said, "I do not so much value a kingdom in comparison."

"But that," returned Hermia, "is mere nonsense. Besides, it is not the truth."

[169]

"It is a part of the truth. And the other part is, that I prefer to have my successor tested while I yet live," the King had then explained, just after a marriage which, even though it stayed irregular to the rule of the law, produced in any case the most quietly domestic couple in all Melphé. For the ageing King delighted more and yet more in his young wife; and they now lived in rustic seclusion, upon the restrained scale of a burgess who has retired, with a snug profit, from his shopkeeping.

It was not that Ferdinand lacked for affairs. Almost daily the ambassador of some foreign power had to be soothed or swindled in the King's small red salon, for he kept his control of all international concerns. Upon Sunday mornings the King very often conferred with the Druids of Rorn, whom for his own reasons he still hired; and his spies also came to him, each once a week, with their thorough-going reports as to all such matters as interested the sedate bright-eyed old gentleman. Besides that, in unoccupied moments, he now entertained himself with a great deal of desultory gardening. He employed a trowel, he climbed ladders, and he trained vines, nowadays, in a fashion somewhat amazing to witness in a monarch of his advanced years. In fact, said Hermia, he counted the leaves upon every plant in his keeping, every morning; to which the King replied soberly that in no known pursuit was accuracy not a fine virtue.

Yet his main pleasure, and his one extravagance, was his collection of jewels. These he delighted to handle and to rearrange and to increase in number judiciously. Nor did he always, it must be confessed, tell Hermia the exact truth as to what he had paid for his most recent acquisition. She was the most thrifty of housewives; and King Ferdinand felt sometimes, with an undeniable sense of guilt, that if only he had haggled a bit longer with the jewel merchant, he might have made a better bargain.

"Yet why do you need so many jewels, my husband, just to look at and to touch?"

"They are pretty," he replied, simply.

"Yes, but, my dear, they do really cost so much!"

"Not when you consider their innate virtues," the King dissented, with a sort of twinkling gravity. "That bezoar stone, for example, which your Cesario stole from me, and which you still wear with such calm effrontery, will turn red with the

[171]

contact of any poison. It is well worth one's while not to be poisoned, I consider."

"That is not what I meant at all; and as is usual when anybody tries to pin you down, you are beginning to talk some nonsense which has nothing whatever to do with it," says Hermia, with a wife's frankness.

"If you look upon it as mere nonsense, child, then in plain honesty you ought to give back to me at once my stolen property."

And Ferdinand, at that, held out his grasping, stubby hand, palm upward.

Hermia looked at him levelly.

"No," she replied; "I loved Cesario. I shall always wear this ring."

The King grunted. He scowled at her, for a moment, with a sort of rigid malevolence. He reached over, and he patted the back of her hand reassuringly.

"Jealousy," says he, "is a stinking bug in a soft bed. Nevertheless, these poets have no pith to them."

Afterward the King went on talking, with a calmness remarkable to witness. It seemed almost exaggerated.

"The sapphire too," he says, "is very useful against poisons. If a spider be touched with a sapphire, then that spider will die instantly. The sapphire becomes pallid upon the finger of any wife who has been unfaithful, even in her thinking. You would do well to leave my sapphires unmeddled with. Moreover, the sapphire makes a man strong and agreeable of demeanor. All my good looks, my wife, I owe to my fine sapphires, for I have here all four shades of the sapphire, as well as five varieties of the star sapphire."

"But—" said Hermia, as a beginning of unflattering protest.

"And then jasper," the King continued— "jasper preserves its owner from drowning. Now I, as you must permit me to point out, have not ever been drowned."

"But—" said Hermia, yet again.

"No," he replied, firmly; "not ever, in my whole life."

At that, she demanded, frowning somewhat, as if unimportantly puzzled,—

"But what has that to do with it, or at any rate, Ferdinand, I mean, what has it to do with whatever you may be talking about?"

"I am simply reminding, you, my wife, on account of your obvious scepticism, that here is yellow jasper, and dark green jasper, and blue jasper, and black jasper. Here is the brown Egyptian jasper brought to me from the Libyan desert; and red jasper from Löhlbach; and this very fine striped jasper, which I got from Siberia, at not very much more than half its fair price. Now, if I had not had in hand all this jasper, then I might quite possibly have been drowned a dozen times over."

"Nobody," says Hermia, in some indignation, "could ever be drowned more than once. So that which you are saying does not make good sense."

"Calmly and accurately," replied Ferdinand, "you have held up to derision the one small defect in my remarks. And still, you are not the least bit angry with me, you may observe. Well, and that, I have not a doubt, is on account of these turquoises, over here in this corner, which prevent discord between man and wife."

She said, soberly: "I am not angry with you, my dear, because, just here at Sinapoli, and always in your own grave and stupid and profoundly absurd fashion, you are so undeniably an idiot, and a darling likewise."

"The world at large," the old King remarked, "does not utterly agree with you. Outrageous as it may appear, there are in this world some persons who regard me without active affection. There have even been eccentrics who confronted me with out-and-out enmity. Now such of them"—his eyes twinkled—"such of them as are yet able to talk, small spitfire, do not always describe me as either an idiot or a darling."

"But does that matter—between us?"

"No," said King Ferdinand; "it does not matter in the least."

—Whereupon, for no reason at all, he kissed his young wife.

"I forgot, though," said Hermia, smoothing back her hair from about the ears, "and it is simply past endurance, the way people pop in as if the place were an inn, because both Cino and Sacrobosco are waiting for you; and I suppose it means that, as usual, supper will be delayed. Whom are you having killed now?"

"Nobody whom you would know, my child," he replied, speaking half over his shoulder, as the King now locked up his cabinet. "It is merely that the governor of Serli has been selling to my over-ambitious son-in-law the plans of our fort there. I can arrange, with Sacrobosco, within two minutes, for the accession of a new governor. And Cino, of course, is bringing me his weekly report as to Lorenzo. That will not take but a half minute."

"Well—" Hermia said, provisionally. "But do you please remember, my dear, that we have soft crabs to-night. And if you do not eat soft crabs the minute they are put on the table, they get stone cold."

"I fly," said Ferdinand. "I shall make all possible haste. I delight in soft crabs. And so, if the poor fellow is despatched bunglingly, it will be all your fault. Yet I must first weigh our good Cino's report as to how my successor is conducting himself."

XXXIII

Reading this report, the King noted thoughtfully that Lorenzo, since becoming Prince Regent, had exercised a high hand in divers matters, but above all, in his current love-affair. In fact, the very first use made of his enlarged powers had been to appoint Pescaro as Keeper of the Prince's Wardrobe.

Moreover, the Prince gave to Pescaro a charming

residence, upon the Lung' Amio, and the Prince granted to his trusty and time-approved servitor a pension sufficient to maintain the Count's proper estate in the discharge of his new duties.

"In brief, the Prince has, all of a sudden, become peculiarly fond of me," says Pescaro, "now that at long last he has learned to appreciate my virtues."

"Rather, it is my virtue which he appreciates," replied Hypolita, "and which he attempts to suborn thus perfidiously with crude carnal bribes."

"Truly, my pet," returned Pescaro, gravely, "and although my tongue hesitates to offend your ears with any such impropriety, yet I fear the intentions of our new master may have an immoral flavor."

"Nevertheless, Marcello, I shall defy the most smooth solicitings of evil, now that I have learned how noble are the rewards of virtue. This fine large home of ours and your snug salary, you must let me remind you, are both the fair bright fruits of your adored wife's fleshly continence. It is sheer virtue, my darling, which has raised us so far beyond Vivaldi and his trumpery sapphires. So do you have faith in me, my dear! and as you go out, remind Assunta to fetch up a slice of onion."

"You are wholly wonderful," Pescaro observed, with conviction. "Like Solomon, my adored one, I now exult in possessing a wife's whose price, to-day at any rate, is far above rubies."

After that, he kissed her in sincere tenderness; and he departed, leaving her guarded only by her own purity.

XXXIV

Somewhat later in this same afternoon, when Pescaro had gone to his new duties at the Governor's Palace, and when Hypolita, in such light clothing as the recent warm weather had made natural enough, was half dozing upon a couch in her bedroom, the extent of her amazement and of her horror to find that Prince Lorenzo had entered her bedroom, is not easy to describe. But the exhibit was wholly convincing, and in fact, for one unguarded moment, it was indiscreet.

"Oh, my prince," then cried Hypolita, drawing upward her pink dressing-gown, so as to cover her most lovely breasts, "but what is it you seek in this place?"

"Love," returned Lorenzo, coming straight to the point, with that candor which befits a prince.

Approaching her, he now took her hand, kissing it ardently; and he placed himself beside her, upon the couch, in an attitude which combined comfort with intimacy.

"Love must have been granted to you at first glance, I think"—Hypolita replied, sighing,—"by all women that have ever seen you. Yet my virtue constrains me—"

"Hah, lady, but who spoke of virtue?"

"I, sir," she returned, in resolute tones; "for you have intruded into my bedroom treacherously; and I can but entreat you to withdraw, out of respect to my honor."

"My dearest, you shall have honor beyond all women in Melphé when you are safely sheltered by my protection."

"You speak with a sweet reasonableness, my prince, and I hear your soft voice with delight. But I hear also the stern voice of my conscience, telling how very black is the sin to which you tempt me."

From that he dissented somewhat, saying, "Even though it were as black as jet, or as ebony, or as the raven's wing—"

"How wonderful it is of you, my prince," remarks Hypolita, in rapt admiration, "to think of so many comparisons so quickly!"

"—Still," he continued, exceedingly well pleased with her and with himself also, "black is the garb of aged persons alone; and we are yet young."

"Black is the garb of all them that mourn, my dear lord; and I fear that I shall always lament your coming hither to-day."

"But I too intend," the Prince assured her, "to repent by-and-by for our shared indiscretion. Yes; for a prince owes it to his people to set them a good example when once he is old enough to make all his doings appear venerable. Meanwhile, we are as yet young, Hypolita; we touch each other, thus longingly, without any least hindrance except your most foolish modesty. Our bodies throb with young blood and with aching, very strong desires. My sweet, you are mine. You shall be mine always. If God dared to come between us now, I would strike Him down!"

"Still, you speak wickedness, my prince," she reproved him, with benign dignity; "and you, whose noble bearing had once led me to believe you an angel of light, are now confessed, even by your own lips, to be a spirit of darkness."

He returned: "I speak truth; and since when has candor become a sin? At all events, for the pleasing iniquities of our youth there will be ample time to repent, in the more temperate season of our old age, when a suitable contrition will be undisturbed by any power to repeat them. Meanwhile, we are young; we are alone; this place is secret; and you lack any defences."

"You mistake, sir; for at all times an honest woman is defended by her virtue."

He shrugged then, saying: "Eh, as virtue goes, you outrival Lucrece. That is granted. But I, my dear, I approach you in the dark rôle of Tarquin. And so the sweet outcome of my most horrid villainy in this bedchamber must be not at all your fault—nor my fault, either, for that matter,—but only the fault of that most bright and bewitching and resistless beauty which Heaven gave you."

"Now but indeed, sir," cried out Hypolita, in perplexed disapproval, "but I wonder that you should dare to speak of Heaven at such an instant."

"I speak in mere gratitude, my adored one, because I am now about to delight suitably in the fair

masterwork of Heaven, and to employ every bit of
it for its planned purpose."

Trembling from head to foot, Hypolita attempted to evade his but too obviously revealed
ardors, by half arising from the couch, and from
his detaining hot grasp. She said, in frightened and
broken accents,—

"If it be my poor beauty, sir, which impels you
to any such hideous outrages, then I must hide it
away from you always."

"I had sooner let the all-glorious sun be removed
from the firmament," Lorenzo replied, fervently.
"And you, Hypolita, would you indeed be so dis-
loyal as to darken, and to make desolate forever,
the life of your prince?"

"I would incite my prince to remember loyally
his own honor, no less than mine," she returned,
with spirit. "To that which is human in you, O my
dear lord, who are so like a god, I would appeal for
mercy. Of you who are all strong and all powerful, I implore that you should not abuse the most
weak of living creatures, a loving woman."

"So, O most lovely Hypolita," says he, in triumph, "and do you confess that you regard me
with unwilling affection?"

The Prince saw that the distraught lady was now aghast by her involuntary admission of a sentiment which, to her unworldly innocence, appeared sinful. Hypolita passed her white fingers about her yet whiter brow, in a despairing effort to collect her scattered senses. She said, trembling but resolute:

"You have taken my heart, ruthlessly, at my first sight of your manly graces. Yet, ah, dear lord, you must permit me to retain my honor! for though my frail woman's flesh be wax to the print of love, yet is my resolve as an honest wife all iron."

The simplicity, in common with the terror, of her appeal thrilled him piercingly; and Lorenzo was moved now by the depth of Hypolita's anguish. He was awed, indeed, by this blinding noble glimpse of her tormented but unshaken virtue in a distress so great. Before her bright purity, his lusts fled; in thought, as well as upon his body's knees, he abased himself before her, detesting his own foulness: and with a large deal of honest remorse the good-hearted, plump Prince cried out, in repentance, to Hypolita.

"Sweet saint," says he, "if I have sinned in fancy, yet do you forgive me in mercy! Do you not curse me, but do you rather revile those fair perfections which have misled me into offending against your chastity! Do you demand vengeance, not against Lorenzo, but against your own loveliness,—yes, and against your own virtue also, for it is my sole sin that I have loved both immoderately."

"Surely, sir," she observed, as if yet in some doubt of him, "if you indeed loved my virtue, you would not attempt to destroy it?"

"Chaste and fair seraph," he replied, reverently —and thus speaking, the Prince arose to his feet— "may it, and you also, live forever in untroubled blessedness! For I now stand before you defeated by your virtue and wholly repentant."

"Yet do you repent at heart, my prince, or but out of some shrewd evil policy?"

"I repent at heart, my all-incomparable angel; and that I shall molest you no more, I make a solemn oath, even by your own pure heart, which flutters under my devout hand, here in its soft white rounded shrine, tipped with a cherry—"

"My dear lord," Hypolita responded, timidly, "I am like blind Isaac: for I hear the smooth, bland voice of too-pious Jacob, but feel the hand of marauding Esau."

"To the contrary, dear lady, it was indeed Jacob who wrestled with an angel."

"Yes, my prince; but that was at Bethel, whereas we, as I must remind you, are virtually in bed."

"It was at Peniel," the Prince corrected her; "although I grant you that when an angel is thus near to one, then all places become paradise."

"Yet to us, dear lord, who are already married, an entrance into paradise is forbidden. So you must promise not ever any more to offend me by talking about love, or by unwise dear thoughts as to our love-making."

"Most solemnly do I swear it, even by the sweet shrine of love—"

"Highness," replied Hypolita, grasping his hand with a respectful ardor, "you are my heart's monarch. Your kingdom does not extend further."

"But I now regard you," Lorenzo explained, "with a purer worship, and with unstained friendship."

"These sentiments are most piously expressed, my prince; I applaud them with a lively gratitude; but still again, I must remind you that the functions of true friendship are less explorative. I am not, I trust, unduly strait-laced. Yet so long as your revered wife is denied her well-earned celestial rewards, and so long as my harsh husband is reprieved from his equally well-earned punishment in realms very far from celestial, your friendship remains the foe of my honor."

She paused, with some eloquence.

"Hah!" said the Prince.

He too, of a sudden, was silent. He said, then, consideringly,—

"Hoh!"

—In reply to which, Hypolita wailed, "I am the most unhappy of living women!"

"Now, but indeed, Hypolita," says he, "it is a vast pity that we are not wholly free to follow the dictates of friendship."

"How utterly would I love you in that event," she returned; "for I would then be the most happy of living women, when once we were free, free of them both!"

He asked—and he still spoke in very quiet, reflective tones,—

"Just what do you mean, sweetheart?"

"I mean that I shall not ever be free, O king of all men," she replied, kissing him passionately, "from my love of you. And yet I must resist that improper emotion. I cannot ever yield to the sin of breaking my marriage vows. I dare not risk my immortal soul through any such dear wickedness. That, O my darling, is what I mean; and I mean every word of it, too! I mean that, so long as either one of them lives, I must keep my virtue unstained by avoiding you forever, after this final farewell kiss. So do you go away now; and do you leave me to my life-long desolation."

Having uttered these impassioned remarks, in a tone which attested the depth of her agony, Hypolita caught up her handkerchief; and the distressed lady began to weep, very pitiably, through the aid of that slice of onion which she had concealed in her handkerchief.

Lorenzo, whom her kisses had set afire, and whom her misery had moved beyond words, attempted to console his adored saint, tacitly, through such methods as occurred to him out-of-hand. It was then that, without speaking, and still sobbing quietly and broken-heartedly, Hypolita with an unrestrained vigor boxed his plump jaws.

—Whereafter Lorenzo gave in. As a reigning prince who had visited a number of yet other bedrooms, he inferred that a gentlewoman who boxed his jaws must be actuated by strong motives of sincerity. In consequence, it was in a chastened mood, and still somewhat reflectively, that Lorenzo kissed the fair hand which but a moment since had set his ears to buzzing. Then without further protest, the Prince departed, toward his new home, in the Governor's Palace.

XXXV

"I have done wrong," said Lorenzo, addressing his wife in tones of sincere contrition, and gingerly rubbing the left side of his face, which still tingled where Hypolita had struck him. "I have been guilty of many faults toward you, my dear Giovanna; but I wish to alter all this. Let us begin a new course of life, and live entirely for each other."

"In that case," says the Princess Giovanna, "what is to become of your Greek strumpet?"

"Why, I can but promise you, my dearest—"

"Promises are all very fine hearing unless one happens to be a married woman. For you break your promises, Lorenzo, and if anywhere in all Melphé there is one single solitary person who doubts that fact—"

"My darling, pray do not excite yourself! Would

you have me make oath before a notary, then, as to my complete devotion henceforward to the sweet solace of your unequalled beauty, and your lively wit, and your amiable disposition?"

"A most solemn oath, Lorenzo. For here, in this golden case, is the charred toe-nail of your own heavenly intercessor, St. Laurence, and it is upon this sacred relic that you must make your oath. Breaking that oath, you will be damned eternally."

Lorenzo had turned pale. This was not at all like swearing by the pure heart, or by any other possessions, of Pescaro's wife. Yet the Prince laid his hand upon the reliquary, and he said, boldly:

"By the toe-nail of St. Laurence, my darling, I swear that never during the rest of your life—or at any rate, not ever of my own accord—will I either see or speak with Madonna Hypolita. So now let us go to my bedchamber."

"That is all you ever think about. You men are all alike," declared the Princess, reprovingly.

She went with him, nevertheless; and to the ardors which Hypolita had kindled, the Princess Giovanna submitted her lean body, at first with a sort of resigned cool patience.

But to-night she found her husband astounding, and his fond caresses to be beyond belief in their liberality. She told him so, with admiring affection; and by-and-by drowsed off into satiated oblivion.

When once Giovanna was sound asleep, then Lorenzo slipped about her long skinny neck the silken noose which he had ready in the pocket of his dressing gown, and he strangled her quietly. Later he called out for help; and her physicians duly certified that the Princess had died of an apoplectic stroke induced by the amorous excesses of a reconciliation with her husband.

XXXVI

Well, and Pescaro was found in an alley-way, upon the next morning but one, very tidily disposed of, with only a single dagger thrust, delivered through his left ribs from behind. It was an affair in which no expense had been spared. Hypolita had retained the great Sacrobosco himself, because of her loyal desire to share at once, and to the full in Lorenzo's bereavement,—as she explained frankly to the sympathizing assassin. Since her unfortunate Prince (that paladin without any equal, whom she confessed to be her heart's sole master) had entered into the forlorn estate of widowerhood, she elected, without any ignoble hesitating, to become a widow;

and in this way to be made no less miserable than was Lorenzo.

"Your sentiments," observed Sacrobosco, as upon her fair pink-and-white fingers he let fall the tribute of three respectful tears, "are a credit to human nature; and I delight to hail, in a client, so much of beauty, of virtue, and of heroism. It is the main drawback to my profession, in this selfish and greedy world, madonna, that I am not invariably retained by perfection."

"No, my good friend," Hypolita replied, modestly; "you must not thus flatter me. I am not perfect; nor do I pretend to be perfect. It is merely that I try to perform my duty as I see it, even at the cost of some self-sacrifice."

The kind-hearted lady sighed then, because, in her forgiving genial way, she rather deeply regretted the loss of Pescaro now that he was virtually buried. She liked the bland, brutal rascal; for the Count understood Hypolita; and, indeed, understood so thoroughly that he was already in flight from his wife when Sacrobosco overtook him.

Yes; for when poor Marcello had heard of how the dear Princess had been called to her heavenly home,—thought Hypolita, with a motherly sort of tenderness,—then he had at once comprehended he

[191]

too would have to be put out of the way. With the cool glance of an expert, he had seen that, for an honorable Christian woman who had sworn to obey and love him alone until death parted them, there was no course left open save to procure his departure out of living.

If only it had been convenient (the distressed widow's thoughts ran on) how gladly she would have spared her Marcello, and have sent him into some sort of quiet exile, on a modest pension! That too, it was to be hoped, he had comprehended. But then, of course, he had comprehended this much, beyond any doubt! A nobly-born person of his nimble discernment must have understood, even during the momentary discomfort of his assassination, that no personal ill feelings were involved, but only the inflexibility of court etiquette. It was out of the question, and indeed it would have been openly scandalous, for a Princess of Melphé to have another husband living. In the exalted circles which Hypolita was now entering, one at every turn had to weigh the obligations of one's position, and one was forced to avoid an appearance of evil.

She yielded therefore to convention; ordered a superb tomb for Pescaro, with eight weeping angels, immediately after breakfast; and before dinner (in the apt phrase of Barnacus), "after having repaid the skill of Sacrobosco with silver, she remunerated the solicitations of Lorenzo with acquiescence." She accepted, in brief, that public marriage which the Prince Regent was now able, at long last, without any further impediment, to offer to the woman whom he loved, as the due reward of her obdurate virtue.

"So my successor has been tested," was King Ferdinand's verdict when he heard about that marriage.

[193]

PART FOUR: THE HEART OF HERMIA

XXXVII

"So my successor has been tested," remarked old Ferdinand, not unaffably, "and Lorenzo fails me."

He ceased then. And the infirm King fell into a brief period of meditation, after having thus voiced an opinion which, nowadays, among the better people of Melphé, was but a little more rare than thrift or virginity.

"For the court of Prince Lorenzo"—as has been recorded, in another place, by the Abbot of Tarba —"displayed, with a bright opulence which beggared the ambitious pen of the toiling historian, such splendors as could not but enchant the beholder and extinguish the voice of unfriendly criticism; delighting as it did alike the heart of the thoughtless pleasure-seeker, of the esurient courtier, of the talented artist, of the pander, and of the thrifty merchant, with an equal profusion; and evoking the muttered envy of less fortunate rulers."

That is as it may be. It is certain that King Ferdinand, in his inglorious retreat at Sinapoli, had been well-nigh forgotten by his nominal subjects, now that (as Thomas of South Miradol puts it) "Lorenzo held in one hand the reins of empire and in the other an ever-open purse." So the Prince Regent continued to become more and yet more popular, in an exact ratio to his unthrift. "Endowed with much natural generosity, and incited hourly by the innumerable graces and the lively exhortations of his wife"—thus Barnacus phrases the matter,—"this prince expended the riches of Melphé with a lavishness thitherto unexampled in the annals of his lately acquired kingdom; for the Princess loved every kind of magnificence, and the Prince Regent continued to worship her with a singular intensity."

Meanwhile, the triumphant climax of their love story had delighted every degree of their subjects, through its wholesome blending of respectability with high-hearted romance. People everywhere liked thus to behold, in real life, and performed by flesh-and-blood actors, a defeating of all harsh enmities—such as they themselves had encountered, only too often, in the unamiable form of super-

fluous spouses and the police regulations—in order
that a shared desire to share the same bed might
get its indulgence properly hallowed, at long last,
by the time-approved benedictions of both law and
religion. It was as good as a novel, said the romantic-
minded; to whom the more realistic had answered
that in any event it helped trade. So had Melphé
rejoiced over Lorenzo's second marriage, and over
his virtual elevation, if always under the small
white thumb of Hypolita, to the throne of Melphé.

For here, as his courtiers now remarked daily, was
no piddling skinflint of a ruler forever troubling
over the exact balance between his treasury and
his debts. Here was one blessed with the far larger
view that posterity might, quite possibly, straighten
out, by-and-by, the obligations of Melphé, somehow, in whatsoever fashion might best suit the convenience of posterity, if, when, and as, the need
to do anything at all did ever become unavoidable.
Here, in fine, as King Ferdinand's successor, had
ascended a more great-hearted and a more gracious
prince who spent his revenues like the base trash
which mere money must always remain to the far-
seeing statesman. "It is the deficit of to-day," Lorenzo was used to declare, "which is making possi-

[199]

ble the surplus of to-morrow." And this sound principle of economics was applauded by every one of his barons who enjoyed a state pension.

Besides that, Lorenzo did not ever bother the nobility by so far debasing himself as to spy on their private affairs. He treated all high-born persons with the frank large confidence which an overlord ought loyally to show in his sworn lieges, without prying into rude and, no doubt, malicious rumors as to the tyranny, or the rapines, or the extortions, practised on their feudal estates,—and in districts which, at all events, were so far removed from Lorenzo that whatever went on there could not rationally concern his comfort, either one way or the other. As a gentleman of the polite world, Lorenzo had not any call to be interested in these rural scandals.

Nor did the Prince Regent ever annoy his officials by checking over their accounts in the mercantile and low-minded manner of King Ferdinand. Lorenzo did not like arithmetic, because it tended to make his head ache. To the blank sordidness of arithmetic he very much preferred the hazy benevolence which he got, nowadays rather too frequently, out of a bottle; and he liked also the amenities of

good talkers and of musicians and of fine works of
art, in admiring which one was backed by depend-
able critics. He delighted, in brief, as a civilized
prince ought to do, in magnificence and in parade
and in royal ceremonies and in sound wine, rather
than in suspecting his most faithful servitors, without any least possible warrant, of swindling him,
and in then proving the swindle.

For the rest, the Prince Regent, it was true, did
not support mistresses in the style to which Melphé
had been accustomed, because in no place could he
find any woman so desirable as in his own bedroom
he found Hypolita. But in all other respects he ful-
filled every duty of his station, and he, in consequence, was acclaimed nowadays as the best-loved
overlord ever known in Melphé.

If Lorenzo was popular, his wife was adored. In
the first place, the Princess Hypolita was beautiful,
with an indisputable and pre-eminent loveliness in
which her people gloried and took a sort of national
pride. She was kind-hearted also, almost beyond
human belief. That fact was notorious. Whatsoever
office or appointment any fairly well-to-do person
desired, he could now obtain, through the kind-
heartedness of the Princess Hypolita, after a private

interview in which she demanded no large bribes, but received graciously every tribute of a loyal postulant which took the substantial and pleasing form of jewelry. Hypolita, indeed, so much delighted in these bright tokens of her subjects' esteem that for a mere bracelet, or for a fine ring somewhat out of the ordinary, she would herself see to it that the desired post was made vacant without any inconvenient delay. She now maintained her personal chemist, Guidobaldo the Panian, who—in addition to preparing her cosmetics and her essences and her unguents and her tooth-powder (which he made of coral and seed pearls) and her hair-washes and her bland bleaches for the complexion—had acquired, moreover, in all branches of toxicology a distinguished efficiency. Yet, here again, the Princess remained as moderate as she was kind-hearted. Hypolita did not ever employ these deadly arts at random, or through mere malice; and had become far too good-tempered, under the genial influences of prosperity, ever to poison anybody except for the sake of some undeniable and rather large gain, or in a case of necessity.

Such cases she could not always avoid. Upon several occasions, for example, she had taken a lover, now that the chance of her having a son by Lorenzo continued to grow more unlikely. Melphé very much needed an heir; and Hypolita, even apart from her ardent patriotism, had every personal prompting to secure her own future by supplying that heir. She remained barren, however, after trying all known remedies and some dozens of the younger courtiers and even—so great was her public spirit—three broad-shouldered grooms from the palace stables.

Well, and these ineffectual collaborators the Princess did, of course, dispose of through Guidobaldo's adroit aid, because that was the most simple, as indeed it was the one infallible, way to ensure their discretion about her self-sacrifice. No man, and in particular no young gentleman who had been reared on the best-thought-of principles, could be trusted out of one's sight, as Hypolita had well learned through experience; and it would not do to have any loose talk smirching the fair name of a princess of Melphé now that all Melphé thrived resplendently.

"Indeed this epoch"—in the words of still another historian—"forms one of those scanty portions in the history of mankind, on which we may

dwell without weeping over the calamities, or
blushing for the crimes, of our species; and ac-
cordingly, the fancy of most contemporary bards,
expanding in the warm gleams of prosperity, has
celebrated the great and genial reign of Prince
Lorenzo as realizing the most beautiful fictions of
the golden age.''

So all sped very pleasantly in San Marco, where
Lorenzo held his court, and where Hypolita ruled
over both it and him. Melphé, delighted by its gay
new rulers, grumbled but moderately as to the increased taxes, which, after all, were being spent
so as to further everybody's enjoyment. "It is the
deficit of to-day"—repeated the fond subjects of
Lorenzo whensoever their taxes were doubled—
"which is making possible the surplus of to-morrow." And at Sinapoli, like a disheveled and patient and time-battered, gray bird of prey, King
Ferdinand watched all this bright junketing, and
became half forgotten by his people.

Once, it is true, came to San Marco a courier
with the tidings that King Ferdinand had suffered
a stroke of paralysis; and for a brief while, this
salutary smiting down of the wicked had nourished
in the breast of Hypolita a great deal of devout

optimism. But the old villain had recovered, quite brazenly. Beyond dragging his left leg a little when he walked, he remained nowadays well-nigh as vigorous as ever, said the very latest, depressing news from Sinapoli.

Well, but before an outcome of this sort, and at his age too, after those year-long depravities which were a matter of common knowledge everywhere, you could not but wonder, in a wholly respectful way, of course, concerning the inscrutable wisdom of Heaven, as Hypolita was now pointing out to her husband.

One, she continued, had not any least notion of criticizing. One merely wondered. That, and that only, was what she meant. Not for a single, solitary instant would a Christian gentlewoman, who did not pretend to be perfect, but who simply tried to perform her duty as she saw it, venture beyond mere wondering, or say one word more concerning the unpleasant matter, or in fact do anything whatever about it, except perhaps to send down—well, Guidobaldo, it might be, if Lorenzo insisted upon his tactfulness, which the man did have, as there was no denying, now that Lorenzo, who was such a good judge of character, had mentioned it.—Just,

Hypolita added, just in mere courtesy, to find out how the poor dear old gentleman really was getting on after his recent illness. It simply did not seem decent that all those superb jewels should remain in that out-of-the-way place, locked up in four cabinets, where they gave no pleasure to anybody, in the disgraceful keeping of an old goat and his cheap strumpet. Something ought to be done about it at once, if only out of politeness and plain Christian charity, even if Lorenzo did keep on talking until doomsday.

—In reply to which, Lorenzo (who, among his many other salutary ignorances, did not know anything about the toxic arts of Guidobaldo) had praised her adorable thoughtfulness; but had preferred, in his own phrasing, to let sleeping dogs lie. His dear father, Lorenzo continued, was best left alone, because God alone knew what the old devil might do if he thought anybody was trying to meddle with him; and besides that, through Heaven's infinite mercy, the infirm King was not, after all, immortal.

So one must have patience for a while longer; one could but wait: and a sweet pet would not bother her loving husband about still more jewelry, not at any rate just for the present, with the kingdom's treasury in a condition which, the more carefully you looked at it, seemed steadily worse.

XXXVIII

Meanwhile—let it be repeated—at the selfsame instant, at Sinapoli, King Ferdinand was saying:

"So my successor has been tested; and Lorenzo fails me. Something will have to be done about it, Hermia, even though you do keep on talking until doomsday."

"Indeed, but it was not right of him," replied Hermia, still intent upon her slow, careful sewing, "to murder his wife."

"No, not in abstract principle, to be sure," the old King agreed, just as absent-mindedly—but looking up now, from his papers, so as to appraise his own pre-occupied staid wife, from over the top of his large reading glasses. "Still, that was managed discreetly; and she was not an attractive young person. One could have forgiven that. It was merely a confession of personal weakness, since in this world the well-balanced man will more or less put up with his wife, when once he has contracted her, without any crude resorting to murder. No, my dear; it was, instead, through his chivalrous conduct afterward, and through his honorable marriage with your handsome and pleasure-loving sister, that Lorenzo has courted his own destruction over-ardently. Hermia, I do not regard that woman with unbridled affection."

Hermia answered him with some sadness.

"Nor does she like us. Now that Hypolita has become a respectably married princess, she declines to have any dealings with the King's whore."

"Tut, child, but she calls me a doddering old lecher, and a swindling lickpenny, and yet a number of other regrettable things—all which I hold listed here, by the bye,—if you come to the high-minded excesses of her respectability. The exuberancies of shrill virtue hurt nobody. No: the true trouble is that she controls Lorenzo. So they live handsomely, wastefully, without governing. He has no head for business affairs, no more than his father had; he stays always half befuddled through his continual wine-swigging: and in all matters she leads him by the nose."

At this point, the King of Melphé rubbed his own nose, with an air of frank irritation.

"And what"—but here Hermia paused, to re-thread her needle—"what have you decided to do about it?"

"I have not wholly made up my mind," he answered, pensively. "I dislike having any near acquaintances killed. With strangers, of course, there is not any personal element involved. But I have not ever been able to avoid a certain feeling of self-consciousness when it came to killing anybody whom I had known, more or less, for some while. Yet what choice have I, Hermia? for all falls into ruin under his slackness and her greedy intermeddling. She exhibits a fair amount of good sense, I must admit, in trying her night-long best to beget an heir for Melphé, and in poisoning off her young lovers afterward, very often even before breakfast. I do not mind allowing her that much deserved praise, because I try always to be just. But your sister is not just. She takes bribes. No ruler can afford to take bribes, because his servants will at once follow his example. And then what have you?—you have at once, you have everywhere, confusion and inefficiency. Why, but I hold here a report as to the late mismanagement of the police department of Bescaglia—"

"Then please do not read it to me, my husband, for I have not ever been able to understand these official matters."

The King looked at his young wife somewhat fondly. He asked, with his old bright eyes twinkling over his reading glasses:

"Would you like better this report as to the increasing corruption of our courts of law? She has been peddling judicial appointments quite as if they were so many cabbages."

"No, my dear," Hermia replied, placidly, as she went on with her sewing, "I do not think I would like it one bit better."

"—Or of the army? or this memorandum as to the pitiable muddling away of our naval stores? or the list of our proposed new taxes? or the millinery bills of the Princess Hypolita? or for that matter, an estimate of the amount which the woman has wasted upon jewelry? It was only last week that her agent overbid my agent on a pair of pomegranate-colored rubies from Ceylon which I especially wanted."

"I remember, my dear. That was the day you threw your inkwell at your agent, and broke two panes of glass out of the window, in your bad temper."

"Well, but what else was I to do, when I can hardly rise up from out of my chair?" asked the King, reasonably. "I wanted those pomegranate rubies from Ceylon. I had meant to place them here, between my four pigeon-blood rubies from the Mogok mines and my two garnet-colored rubies from Siam. But Hypolita got them! The woman has not any sense of decency."

"Still—" said Hermia.

"No, child, you are quite wrong. I am speaking logically; and women have not any sense of logic, either. I hold here all the proofs of her wickedness, all written down neatly by my spies, with every enormity dated even to the half-hour. And all fits together. All is slackness, waste, inefficiency, extravagance—and in brief, all works toward ruin. The kingdom which I created begins to collapse, under the mismanagement of Sigismund's good-hearted and open-handed and easy-going bastard. Lorenzo maintains virtues which no king can afford."

"And what do you intend doing," asked Hermia, "to put down this alarming display of virtue? For of one thing you may rest assured, my dear, and it is that I shall not permit you to leave this house until your walking is better."

"Do you stop bullying me, small spitfire! Now that I have suffered this second stroke, my walking will not ever be better. We both know it. My body is done for."

"Why, but the doctors say——"

"Of course they do: that is what they are paid for. Nevertheless, and body or no body, I remain King of Melphé. Moreover, I am, in my way, an artist. From out of the bleak wreck which was left by Sigismund, I had builded a contented and strong and thriving kingdom. Some of it I stole with Carneschi's assistance, some of it I stole unaided: but all of it I made better. I do not defend my creative methods; I point instead, with the quiet vainglory of a self-satisfied artist, toward my work. I made Melphé. Under my rule, the barons grumbled, just as they formed plots to assassinate me, through mere force of habit, for they were not really dissatisfied. Trade prospered. We builded finer churches, five nunneries, new brothels, seven great bridges, superb public privies, a couple of universities, and excellent roads. The common people, even the poorest of them, had food and homes and some happiness."

Old Ferdinand paused here. He moistened his lips.

"Now," he said, harshly, "now my kingdom breaks up under your cooing, gushing, tender-voiced sister's misrule. The Prince squanders. The barons begin to play the petty tyrant, openly. They override my laws. Bribery becomes as general as breathing. The King's justice does not approach everyone of my subjects equally. Very soon the commoners will have drifted back into their old cowed slavery; and Melphé will not any longer be a fine and well proportioned work of art. But I will not have my work ruined by a fat fool's heroic devotion to his own lawful wife!"

"So what follows, my husband?"

"Well," says the King, considerately, "well, now, that lean-jawed Cesario of yours was not a fool of this special sort."

"No," says Hermia.

"Your face reddens, my dear. Do you find the room too warm?"

"No," says Hermia.

"I mean," the King explained, "that the jack-

anapes was too utterly given over to self-love ever
to be misled very dangerously by his love for any
woman breathing."

"Why, but indeed, my husband, I have some reason to agree with you."

"So it would be well, perhaps, if we could have
back Cesario."

"Nobody knows where he is."

"That fact is news to me," says the King, a degree frostily.

"So then, Ferdinand"—she spoke quickly—"then
you do know! And you have known for ever so
long, I have not the least doubt. Yet not one single
word of it did you ever see fit to mention to me!
And all I have to say is—!"

"—Perhaps better left unsaid," the King suggested. "Yes, I have known for some while. My
curiosity is considerable. But, to the other side, so
is my selfishness. You have made me content, small
spitfire. Never in my life had I been quietly content until I had dragged you down into the riotous
excesses of our immorality, and into that wild
flaunting life of sin, here among my account keeping and your needlework, about which your pious
sister—in those pomegranate rubies which she vir-

tually stole from me—cannot speak without tears. So I did not want Cesario back, because you still love Cesario."

"I wonder if I do?" replied Hermia, quite placidly. "I was heart-deep in love with him, once, of course. But all that seems so very far away, and so unimportant, nowadays."

"That I believe to be as near the truth as any woman can venture with comfort. Yet it is not the complete truth, you tiny vixen."

"Perhaps it is not," she admitted. "But, O my gruff, dear, snarling pest of a husband! and do you doubt my affection for you?"

"I would sooner doubt the existence of—well, not of God, it may be. I have not ever been much thrown with Him. Let us say of the Devil. Still, I did not wish the Druids of Rorn to fetch back Cesario during my lifetime. On the contrary, I have paid them not to molest him. But in this world we cannot all have all our preferences. My life is now near its end. I must put my affairs in order. I have but two, or it may be three affairs which I value. I value Melphé, and you, and my trinkets yonder in the way of gems. When I am gone—wheresoever one does go after death, Hermia,—then not only the Melphé which I created, but you also, my dear wife, and what is far more dangerous, your jewels likewise, will be at your sister's disposal. That arrangement does not suit me. I must prevent it."

"But what possible means can you employ?"

The old King took off his reading glasses and laid them on the table. His lips curdled with a soured but triumphant smiling.

"My instrument, child, now scowls in the doorway."

Hermia looked up then, to find Cesario standing there.

XXXIX

Cesario was not pleased; and through an aloof combining of the scornful with the sullen, his face had betrayed as much. He waited in the doorway, as yet silent; but he now regarded Ferdinand with the air of an angel who considers an insect.

The old gentleman leaned back in his chair. Across the white expanse of the numerous, neatly assorted papers upon his writing table, he scowled up at Cesario, appraisingly, without speaking.

But Hermia had arisen, with a half stifled cry;

her sewing scattered everywhither, so untidily that a scrap of snipped-off linen still adhered to her brown skirt, now that she came straight to Cesario; and her lifted face was both glad and tender.

The King cleared his throat.

"You can now see, my dearest," said old Ferdinand, wrily, "that you, in point of fact, did not tell me the exact truth. However! that does not matter now. Do you welcome our glum guest civilly, but without—if I may venture a suggestion— quite so many amorous ecstasies. And do you then go away, for I have need to talk with Cesario, and my time is short."

Hermia said: "But, Cesario! Cesario, how you have changed! You are as handsome as ever, my dear, but you are so lean and pale! and so very cross looking!"

"Time does not beautify every mortal person," Cesario answered her, in the polite tones of apology; "nor does everybody delight thus to be meddled with by the brutal and hog-like stupidity of a browbeating and infirm old mule."

"Eh?" says the King.

"Oh, but, sir," Cesario exhorted him, "do not be perturbed as to my discretion! It is firm-set.

I quite comprehend that I am forbidden to mention any names, alike by my fond loyalty as a subject, and by my natural affection as a supposed son of this mule."

"You reassure me," says the King; "and I have now indeed no least doubt remaining as to your discretion."

About Hermia the mocking glance of Cesario slipped coldly, yet again. He said:

"Beyond question, time has changed me, yonder. But time and yet other forces, I discover, have been hard at work, hereabouts, to help your advancement in all respects. It follows that I do not clearly recognize the small shy girl whom I left—and whom I left sworn to eternal fidelity, madonna, —in that handsome, if perhaps rather plump, stepmother whose hand at this instant I am kissing with all suitable deference. It is most gratifying, in passing, to observe that you still wear the ring with which you married me also. Your constancy affects me."

Her lips had quivered somewhat: otherwise, she did not move at all. It was as if Hermia, after having been lashed once with a whip, and being fettered, awaited merely a second blow. She did not answer Cesario.

Instead, it was the old King who now snarled like an enraged beast. He spoke then, gratingly. He said:

"Have patience. I shall be gone very soon. Meanwhile, Cesario, you must not make love to my wife before my face. Go away for a little while, my dearest. You turtle-doves will have time in plenty, by-and-by. But I have no time. I have merely a strong need to talk privately with our runagate cool phrase-making cardinal."

"I am at your service, sir," said Cesario.

"Then do you stop gritting your teeth at me! for you are far more at my service than you suspect. I have work for your Eminence. Shut the door."

Ferdinand was obeyed; but then, to the former squire of Arvieto, that was not any longer a novelty.

XL

"Now then, Cesario," said the King, briskly, "to begin with, I am dying."

"I, sir," the younger man replied, "in common with all Melphé, cannot, of course, but regret your sad news suitably."

He was repaid with a scowl which was like a dark brooding thunder-cloud of contempt and of indignation, as yet dubiously restrained.

"Phrase-making, Cesario," says the King, "is a gift with its not negligible value. Yet you misuse that gift. It enables you, for example, at this present instant, to condescend languidly toward me in my body's feebleness. You are pleased to avail yourself of the privilege. That does not matter. My skin is thick. But, a minute ago, this gift enabled you, also, to hurt Hermia, with your polite sneer as to her 'eternal fidelity' after you had deserted her."

With that, the old fellow struck his fist upon the table; and under his shaggy brows his eyes blazed. Cesario found that, without knowing it, he had stepped backward before the blare of a large malignity, like that of lightning. Ferdinand said,—

"You have hurt Hermia!"

Then, just as suddenly, the old King controlled his fury. His wrinkled hands gripped each other. About his thick white hair you could see the sweat-beads a-sparkle. And Ferdinand went on speaking, in deliberate harsh tones.

"You may well praise whatever gods you have learned to worship in your Branlon, Cesario, that my first duty is toward Melphé. As a private person, I have no rights. Well, and to the other side, as a king, I have no compunctions. For that reason I have hired the skill which makes all-powerful against your Branlon the earnest-minded Druids of Rorn. For that reason I have drawn you back, out of your trumpery magic-haunted Branlon, just as an angler draws a trout from the water, because Melphé has need of you. So do you sulk if you like, Cesario! and do you drawl out your barbed phrases if that at all comforts you! Nevertheless, I am stronger than you are; and it is my will that you should serve Melphé."

Cesario answered him, with a coolly elaborated politeness:

"It is to you, sir, that Melphé belongs, as after your all-glorious reign, it will be the kingdom of Lorenzo. I have not any part in its sturdy but, to my taste, somewhat prosaic splendors. I have no least duties toward Melphé."

"To begin with," the King replied, "Melphé is

not only a kingdom, not merely its ruler's gilt play-thing. Melphé is flesh and blood. Melphé is men and women."

"That, sir, I do not dispute," says Cesario, mildly amused by the old rascal's naïveté.

"The men and women of Melphé, the mere run of mankind," said the King,—"it is they whom we have to consider, first, and their poor human needs. It takes so very little to content them. They need only a home and food, a little work, their mates and their children. Out of these simple things, in the ever-present black shadow of chance and of death, they create, very incredibly, their content-ment. So for their sake, Cesario, you must now put aside Branlon, and the fine dreams of your youth, and your rights as a private person to any special happiness, or indeed to any particular virtue."

"Why?" said Cesario, dryly. "But why on earth, my dear sir, need I be paying to iniquity any such large and expensive tribute?"

"Because, my poor boy, you are one of those luckless persons out of whom accident has made a king. So you must learn to lie, and to steal, and to kill—yet always judiciously, and always for your people's profit,—because each of these vices is need-

ful to the beneficent ruler. It would be more pleasant, as beyond doubt it would be more edifying, if
all kingdoms did not remain dependent upon the
wise dishonesties and the thrifty crimes of their
overlords; but, thus far, mankind has not invented
any more efficient method of restraining its own
fond imbecilities. We kings must needs work with
the tools at hand."

Ferdinand was silent for some while. He looked
incredibly tired, Cesario noted. But Cesario said
only, with cool firmness:

"You are talking very infamous nonsense, sir;
and I, if but as a devout clergyman, cannot accept
either your philosophy or your Melphé."

—To which the gray tyrant returned, implac-
ably:

"You have no choice in this matter. You are the
next heir after Lorenzo. His strumpet is not capable
of child-bearing, or he of leaving her. If you do not
take the throne when Lorenzo dies—and I have
reason to believe," the old gentleman remarked,
meditatively, "that he will not outlive me a great
while,—then there is none to inherit after Lorenzo.
Bracciano would claim the throne, in his wife's
right, as my son-in-law. There would be war with

Bracciano. In that futile warring many hundreds would be killed. Of every one of these killed persons you, Cesario, would be the true murderer. Nor is that everything. Among the barons here in Melphé would arise a plotting and a fighting, until some one of these barons had killed off enough of his rivals to grasp the crown insecurely, and to hold it until some other baron had bereaved him of it, along with his life. All would drift back, in brief, into the bleak bright savagery of Duke Sigismund's time; and my Melphé would be destroyed."

Cesario still smiled, rather maliciously.

"Hah, sir, but inasmuch as—I can but repeat—you have seen fit to make of me a clergyman, whose sole interest is in religious matters, and whose restrained small field of exercise is the pulpit, what can I well do in these sad circumstances?"

"In these sad circumstances," Ferdinand replied, with a continued and an all-demolishing lack of irritation, "the Pope has agreed that you may resign your cardinalate."

"Hah!" said Cesario.

"By good luck," the old King continued, "you have not ever taken holy orders. So you must marry now and beget children to reign after you. It has virtually been settled—as I do not mind telling you, Cesario, since it to-day is an open secret—that you are to marry the Princess Christine, the Duke of Lorraine's daughter, the granddaughter to the Queen Mother of France. As yet, we are still arguing over the girl's dowry. It ought to be more than they offer. In addition to 600,000 crowns and the Queen Mother's share of the Medici property in Florence, we must have likewise a formal transfer to your wife of every one of the Medici claims to Urbino. And in the end we will get that."

"All this, then, has been settled by you, even before my return!" says Cesario, giving a loose rein to his fretfulness. "It appears, sir, that by your way of thinking, I alone am to have no say in arranging my own life! and that my happiness matters to nobody!"

"You are quite right in both suppositions," old Ferdinand agreed, placidly, "now that chance and the large folly of Sigismund's bastard are about to make you a ruler over your fellow creatures. So do you stop talking your nonsense about happiness! and do you listen to me—most carefully Cesario,—as to what you must do after my death."

The King spoke then, at some length.

XLI

When the King had ended this speaking, then by the King's orders, old Ferdinand was carried up to the top of his villa. In this place was a sort of canopied roof garden, where he and Hermia had been used to sit, in warm weather, when a breeze came up out of the sea to the east of them. Westward you overlooked the river called Alvia and the broad harbor of Sinapoli.

"I would see my kingdom," says Ferdinand, "for the last time."

So he sat now, leaning back in his tall chair, facing the sunset; and with him were Hermia and Cesario. The old man regarded meditatively the long line of red roofs and of red-capped towers, rising above the sombre green of palm-trees, which formed the river front of Sinapoli. The tide was out; in the brown shining mud below the gray sea-wall, you saw the impatient white moving, the short circling flights, of gulls at their supper. Beyond, all the wide west was gilded with an unvarying and blinding gold.

Now upon the long white Bridge of Lions the

drawbridge was raised, in order to admit the entry of a black-and-red merchant vessel into the harbor. The King, squinting up his tired eyes, asked if this ship did not display the flag of Spain? and was told yes.

He replied, "Our sales to the Spaniards have increased most gratifyingly since the recent trade agreement."

"It is an announcement, sir," says Cesario, "which rouses me to supreme ecstasy."

"We gave them a tariff reduction," Ferdinand continued, heavily, "on forty-seven products, ranging from sixteen to fifty per cent., so nearly as I remember; but in turn, they made reduction upon the fixed price of forty-five of their exports, including raw silk, mules, coal, and carpet wool. All these were necessary to us. Yes; I made a fair bargain."

"Let us hope, sir, that the Spaniards still think so."

The King grunted.

"In fact, I did cheat my illustrious good friend and beloved cousin, Philip, within reasonable limits, for the good of Melphé. I created Melphé. I cannot make phrases about it, Cesario: but in that red and gray and green, quiet city, where now some two hundred shops have just put up their shutters for the night, and where, in the plaza, the town band are tuning their instruments at this very instant, there, during Sigismund's black time, were untilled fields and burned huts and frightened people living desperately upon what they could take by blind force from one another. Now, in place of those naked mud-flats, is Sinapoli, a prospering seaport; and back of it are Melphé and Pania and Ferrata, all blended into one kingdom."

Cesario answered him: "There is union, the union of well herded cattle. There is a degree of contentment. And at this instant, just as you say, sir, your not discontented burghers—now that the day's taskwork, of swindling one another respectably, is finished with,—may sit in the plaza, down there, and they are privileged to listen to an inferior, trivial, catchpenny sort of music. And upon the soiled, ring-stained table before him, each tradesman has a bottle of wholesome enough, if inferior, sour wine, with which to befuddle himself until the Cathedral bell shall have sounded, religiously, the fixed hour for him to trudge homeward, toward the pursuit of staid copulation with his half-asleep and imperfectly washed wife. Quite truly, these civic pleasures are better than are the wild throat-cuttings of warfare. These things are tangible blessings. And bedrugged by them, your loyal subjects can manage to live—just as they do live, sir,—untroubled by high and dangerous dreams such as might discontent your plump shopkeepers with the placid life of well herded cattle."

"Each one of us, my son," says the King, quietly, "has his own dream. Believe me when I protest that I have not any quarrel with the dreams of your lost forest. They are fine playthings for young people, doubtless. But I am not young any longer. I have almost forgotten my brief youth and the clinging soft hands of Maria. I now love better the ever-busy hands of small Hermia."

He paused here. He touched Hermia's hand, but without looking toward her, because his more immediate concern was to save the kingdom which he had created.

"And so,"—the old man continued,—"my dream is different. I cannot make phrases about it, Cesario. But to help human beings some little way toward orderly and contented living, is that not a dream as brave and strange as is any dream of

Branlon? That is what I have done, Cesario, here in my daylit Melphé, in my own commonplace and prosaic decreed kingdom. I have worked with what tools I might, with Holy Church and your mother's whoredoms, with Sacrobosco and with the town band, and with beneficence and treachery also, just as seemed most expedient. I have worked among many infamies, with soiled hands. But I have worked always in the service of my dream, of my own small, unimaginative, sane dream. It has been made tangible through my long labors. Now it is threatened, now it dissolves, before the greed of a light-minded strumpet. And there is no more strength left in me. I cannot serve my dream any more. I cannot even walk from this chair to yonder palm-plant, Cesario. Cesario, my staid strong dream must not perish now that I go down, so very feebly, to my last sleep, beyond the reach of all human dreams!"

"My father," said Cesario, "it shall not perish!"

"Why need you be telling me that?" King Ferdinand grumbled at him,—"when it is what I have been telling you from the very first."

But Cesario went on speaking, in a whirl of words that were half earnest and half scoffing, he could not have said which.

"I have given men songs where you gave them sewerage. Which one of us labored the more nobly? —why, I, sir, beyond doubt, to every appearance. And yet the real point, I think, is that, while my songs were but so-so, your sewers were of the first order. So I must see to it they are kept in sound condition. You bequeath to me, not a sceptre, but a pick-ax; and you put me upon my mettle to show that a minor poet may yet prove a good ditch-digger."

"Phrases! still phrases!" the King said,—"even though, if but for variety's sake, you have flavored them with some little intelligence."

"I blush," returned Cesario, "before the too sweeping terms of your genial flattery; and yet, by and large, I agree with you. By and large, I accept my appointed rôle. You have created, in your Melphé, a strong and irresistible and murderous mechanism. You have given to plain mediocrity its horrible triumph over all poets, over all makers who would make new and more lovely things than earth nourishes. Well, and I—I, who was once a poet of sorts, if but a very minor poet—I must see to it that this triumph continues, in the most high and holy and hideous name of human progress!"

"Nevertheless," said the old King, scowling as if

with extreme malevolence, "you, and you alone of your mother's spawn, have called me your father."

Cesario was honestly startled to comprehend that he had indeed done a thing so incredible. He stammered out:

"You observe trifles, sir. That is a useful accomplishment. It is but that one honors the conventions—"

"No, my son: you have called me your father because, at long last, you know that, whether or not my blood be your blood, yet my work is your work, and my life's need is your final need. Now that you too are not young any longer, Cesario,— and even though, in point of crude, carnal fact," the King said, casually, "it was Carneschi who begot you upon the hospitable, fat, hot loins of my first wife,—now that need is to serve Melphé; and to surrender your own puny, so hungry, human will to the welfare of your decreed kingdom. It is your need, now, not to think any longer about new and more lovely things than earth nourishes. Only the very young are permitted to go into Branlon, or even into places yet more unwholesome, in their quest after such things. We permit that, because they are compelled to come back, by-and-by, empty-handed, and hiding their bruises as they best may. Forever afterward, for the ageing person, Cesario, there is only the choice between mediocrity and destruction. For the ageing person there are no more jaunts into Branlon. The dissenter, the dreamer, the rebel, and the self-sufficient, vainglorious poet—all these, under one or another cloaking, must surrender to the law of Melphé, by-and-by, when youth leaves them, or else perish. You have chosen not to perish. I am glad. In your decreed kingdom there is not any place for the extraordinary person. He upsets matters. So one man out of every hundred, Cesario, the wise prince will make an end of, as mercifully as he can well manage, in order that the prosperity and the peace and the smugness, and the gross needs in general, of some ninety-nine persons may thrive. That is the law of Melphé. That is the law of kings. That is the law of all earth."

Cesario said, "So my true father was Carneschi—whom you caused to be murdered!"

"In that matter I followed your advice, Cesario, your most earnest advice; and for a wonder, you gave me good counsel."

"Yes; I remember, sir. That must have entertained you a great deal, to have me begging you to kill my own father before sunrise."

"The impetuosity of youth, Cesario, does have its amusing aspects now and then," the King admitted, dryly.

"Moreover, sir, as I must make bold to mention, you brought about the death of my mother."

"Both of your parents died," returned Ferdinand, "for the good of Melphé."

"Oh, doubtless!" Cesario agreed. "Yet I do not know but that they died likewise in order to satisfy your malignity and your jealousy of them. I shall not ever know about that. It is the mark of every social reformer to murder off, upon sound civic grounds, all persons who have offended him. So it may be that you are infamous, sir, from every moral and æsthetic standpoint. Still, there is Melphé, where before your time there was only mud with untamed beasts fighting in it. Your sewers are good sewers; and at this instant I believe in their importance."

"Why, then," says the old gentleman, cheerily, "everything is as it should be; and to-morrow may yet prove for Melphé as fine a day as that sunset promises. For my work goes on."

He looked now, at last, toward Hermia, scowling at her.

"I have arranged for Cesario's marriage. You

[234]

have my permission, if you like, to become his mistress. He will be very lonely. He has his better traits. He is not wholly an imbecile. Carneschi has increased my already large indebtedness to Carneschi by providing me with an heir who, at any rate, possesses the intelligence and the cold self-conceit which Lorenzo lacks. And you love Cesario —or so, at least, you believe. I admit I do not think that, at the last pinch, you will be able to endure Cesario. Intelligence is not everything. You will miss those finer qualities of amiability and of tenderness to which I have accustomed you," Ferdinand remarked, with the diabolic grin of a gargoyle.

His wife replied: "Why do you make fun of that which is true? To no woman living has been granted any love more great or more tender than you have given to me, my husband, or I to you, Ferdinand."

The King caught his breath sharply. He moistened his lips, as if in discomfort. He resumed, equably:

"At all events, in my grave I shall not be jealous of your kisses, even though you should elect to squander them upon this foiled minor poet. The dead have not any lips, by-and-by, nor any heart either in their bared ribs. So do you kiss me now, for the last time, my own true tiny wife, while my heart is all yours. Cesario or no Cesario, you have been more dear to me than I have ever dared tell you. It would have embarrassed me. I would say God bless you, if only I were somewhat more certain as to my friendly relations with Heaven. Yet God also is a king. So perhaps He will understand. I have done my work as I best might. And I am tired. I must rest."

"Rest very tranquilly, O my dearest," said Hermia, with her fond arms about him, "for I am now yours, as you are mine, forever."

He smiled at that, saying to her, comprehendingly, and yet with a sort of compassion,—

"These poets, small spitfire! there is no pith to them."

He said then: "Pardon my loquaciousness. In one more moment I shall rest. But this is important, Cesario. That Spanish ship has reminded me of their complaints as to our duties upon wool. They are right; and I had meant to attend to it. Now you must attend to it. Their wool is essential. They are so improvident as to raise merino wool for us, and then to buy back, at our own prices, mind you, the cloths we make out of it. So their wools ought to be admitted duty free. Do you remember, Cesario, as my last word to you, now that I die, there should be no further tariff upon Spanish wools. Then, too, in regard to the allied matter of their wines—"

With that, the old gentleman paused, as if somewhat surprised. His lips parted. You saw he was trying to moisten them, and could not quite manage it.

"But this," he said, in aggrieved protest against the intrusiveness of death, "this is important. In regard to the custom duties upon Spanish wines—"

He breathed sighingly, as if acquiescent, at last, in his own defeat; and his large gray head fell sidewise a little, toward the left. He lifted it, though, rigidly, with an effort very painful to witness; and then lay back, prosaic and grotesque, but erect, in his tall chair, facing the sunset.

In this manner died the first King of Melphé.

XLII

Now Hermia looked up, from the dead body of her husband, toward Cesario. Her eyes were very bright, but tearless.

"He did evil," she said, quietly. "And yet he was good. And I loved him. I did not know until now how much I loved him."

Cesario answered, frettedly: "Well, but I did not love him. I had not any compelling reason to love the murderer of my sister, of my brother, and of both my parents. Moreover, the old swindler would not ever let me live out my life as if it were my life instead of his life. To begin with, he had me made a cardinal when I wanted only to be your husband, Hermia, and when you wanted me to be your husband."

Hermia was regarding him with a sombre and very steady intentness.

"Yes, I can remember that time, Cesario. But how far away my love for you seems now! and how strange!"

"Our adoration for each other was not at all strange," he assured her. "You were a most attractive girl. I was quite fond of you. In fact, I thought that my heart would break when I had to leave you. But if I had not run away at once, then the old man would have made a pope out of me."

"Indeed, Cesario," she returned, without ever shifting her brown sad eyes from his eyes, "I think that in declining to adorn the Christian Church you did only your Christian duty."

"And now"—Cesario continued the dire tale of

his injuries—"when I was getting on quite comfortably as a poet in Branlon, he has fetched me back into his dull, damned Melphé. He has got out of me my word of honor to save Melphé and you. That will detain me here for Heaven alone knows how long. But to cap everything, he has left me uncertain as to whether he was not right from the first. I do not like to have my convictions shaken."

"It seems to me," replied Hermia, still speaking very equably, "that you are now fretting like a spoiled child, because, after you had fallen into an idle and worthless way of living, my husband has put a stop to your childish nonsense."

"I am not sure of that. You do not understand Branlon," Cesario returned, with impatience. "I am sure only that statecraft has dumped me, once more, into the quagmire of practical politics."

She demanded of him, rather tartly, "And what will you, Cesario, what will you, of all creatures, be doing in politics?"

He shrugged, in answering: "Why, now that I have been hauled back, willy-nilly, I must play out the game which the old man has ordered. And the first move in it must be made by Hypolita. Meanwhile, we cannot stand here forever squabbling over his corpse."

"But who started that squabbling?"

"You did," Cesario replied, promptly. "You started it by showing an insensibility which does not at all become a newly-made widow, as you must permit me to tell you, and which could not but irritate any loving son beyond reasonable endurance."

"I did not start it."

"You did start it, Hermia."

"But no! for you started it yourself, Cesario, with your whining, like a great baby, because you were being called on to behave sensibly. And moreover, I would like to know, when did Carneschi's bastard become my dear husband's 'loving son'?"

Cesario began to laugh.

"See now," he said, "see how the old thieving murderer contrives still to part us!"

"Yes," said Hermia, with extreme soberness; "and he will always do that. For it was this old thieving murderer, as you call him, whom I loved truly, because he was great-hearted. He was lonely. He was strong. But you, Cesario, you are not any one of these things. No; it was the plain truth which you told me, so very long ago, on that hot beach where the bright blinding air smelt of seawater and two ospreys were hunting overhead. You are a mere fribble; and there is no depth to you, either for good or for evil."

Saying this, she slipped from off her finger the ring containing the bezoar stone. It had not ever left her finger since Cesario placed it there upon the beach at Gratignolles. To remove it, was the one thing which she had refused to old Ferdinand during his lifetime. She removed it now. She gave back the ring to him who had first placed it upon her finger, reaching out to him over the dead body of her husband.

PART FIVE: THE TRIUMPH OF HYPOLITA

XLIII

Now even in name had Lorenzo become King of Melphé; over Lorenzo ruled Hypolita; and the old King's body, after the embalmers had done with it, was honorably conveyed to the little chapel of Our Lady of the Milk, for the while that his tomb was being made ready in the Cathedral of San Marco.

He lay in state, among an assemblage of very tall, fat candles, wearing a doublet of red satin and hose of the same color. Over these they had dressed him in his purple and gold robes as Grand Master of the Order of San Antonio; upon his breast showed his order of the Golden Fleece; and beneath his stubby folded hands lay an embossed, rather large, jeweled sceptre. He was thus made wholly magnificent; and yet his rough strong face, which seemed so placid, was more than magnificent, somehow: for you saw, now, that Ferdinand dei Vetori had been truly a great personage.

So at least Cesario reflected; and he wondered,

too, if the thrifty old gentleman would have much relished being exhibited in this resplendent condition.

"I did not like you, sir," said Cesario, "and yet I do not hate you either. Once more I discover that my emotions are not rising suitably to the occasion. You brought about directly the death of my mother; my father you caused to be murdered, very hideously, with a deliberated cruelty: and still, I do not think about you with any loathing, or even with active dislike. In point of fact, I am not especially excited, either one way or the other, about the murder of my parents. And you I regard merely with a certain sense of relief that you will not browbeat or swindle me any more. I regard you also with a faint sense of fretfulness, because you have now burdened me with the affairs of your stupid Melphé and of your equally stupid Hermia. And that is all. It is a tiny total which appears enormously inadequate."

And Cesario said likewise: "I should at this very instant, by every rule of the appropriate, be splitting the welkin with wild cries of triumph because the murderer of my parents has gone down into Hell, to suffer there for his unparalleled crimes eternally. To the contrary, with my relief in being rid of your devious ways, and with my fretfulness over the burden which you have put upon me, is mingled a most lively degree of admiration. As much as it troubles me, sir, to admit the fact, I think you were worth a dozen of my parents. I am certain you were worth at least a hundred Cesarios. And so I shall not fail you."

At that, Cesario bent down. He kissed the dead, stubby hand, saying:

"Abominable and prosaic tyrant, your work shall go on. I promise you, sir, that so often as the weather permits, the town band shall continue to play in the plaza."

XLIV

Cesario then went back to Hermia. She had been confined in the convent of the Penitent Magdalene, at Murato, by the new King's orders; and old Ferdinand's great collection of gems had been seized, as being the property of the Crown.

In the convent garden, enclosed steeply upon every side with gray buildings, the small prisoner sat alone, upon a wooden bench that had been

painted gaily in orange-color relieved with touches
of black. She was shaded by some half dozen palm-
trees, in the rough trunks of which many ferns
had found an unaccustomedly lofty rootage. These
ferns trailed downward about the tree-trunks,
almost everywhere, like imponderable vines, waving
delicately. Their more green and more lively graciousness made the palm-branches, above them, appear stiff and brittle and sallow.

Imprisoned Hermia, with her plump back
turned to the sunlight's glare, was about her embroidery quite as if nothing untoward had happened. The doomed woman's prosaic and self-satisfied calm troubled Cesario.

"Well, but all this," says Cesario, half-fretfully,
"was predicted by your late husband. Your marriage to him, being at best a morganatic marriage,
is hallowed by the Church, but stays disputable in
law. It need not be recognized unless Lorenzo
chooses to recognize it. His wife orders him not to
do this. Who is he, to dispute the will of Hypolita?
Why—as you, very justly, have failed to remark—
he is but a mist wreath drifting about the granite
top of a mountain. From these atmospherical reflec-
tions I infer that you may quite legally be locked

up, as a woman of notoriously loose living,—even though I do not imagine that Hypolita has ever weighed this affair in the cool scales of jurisprudence. She has weighed only the fact that, until yesterday, you had in your possession four cabinets brimful of fine gems which she wanted."

Hermia looked up from her embroidery for a brief instant; and said, with a flavor of condonation,—

"But, then, she was always very fond of jewelry."

"That," Cesario agreed, "is the precise trouble."

"And what," asked Hermia, as she went on, still half-abstractedly, with her taskwork, "what, do you think, is to become of me in consequence?"

"Why, on account of her Majesty's refined taste in gems, and on account of her respect for the proprieties, you will be treated with a most remarkable and widely advertised kindness during your imprisonment. You will have every comfort except your freedom; and you will be permitted to live for a reasonable while—even, I imagine, for four or five months. Then you will die on a sudden, either of heart-failure or of indigestion, without causing any least breath of scandal."

"Do you mean poison?" asked Hermia, thoughtfully comparing two skeins of green silk with the background of her embroidery.

"I do," said Cesario; "and so does Guidobaldo the Panian; and so does she."

Hermia decided upon the darker shade of green, and unwound this skein, after having dropped the other one into her work basket. Hermia said, mildly, but with conviction,—

"I do not think that is right of her."

"You have a truly sublime talent for tranquillity, and for meiosis likewise," Cesario remarked, in unconcealed admiration. "You are not ever at a loss for the apt phrase. No; it would not be right of your sister to murder you, now that she holds you here like a trapped sparrow. And yet"—he groaned—"yet you will not even take back our betrothal ring, and so permit me to protect you throughout the remainder of our shared existence. You can see for yourself the ring is entirely too tight for my little finger: nevertheless do you continue to subject me to this manual discomfort, through refusing to show any pity, my adored Hermia, for the inextinguishable love which I have always borne you."

She looked up at him, with a grave smile, saying,—

"Always, Cesario?"

"One cannot prevent, my dear Hermia, an occasional attack of the explorer's ardor," he admitted, reluctantly—"or of a generous inclination to increase the happiness of one's fellow creatures at all times and places, including bedrooms."

"Just so. And therefore, dismissing your life-long fidelity, Cesario, I must tell you, as I have told you over and yet over again, quite apart from the fact you are now going to marry that Princess Christine, who seems really a nice looking girl, but then we all know what those portrait painters are, even with me, and she does do her hair so unbecomingly, I think, because at all events you could not expect me to encourage you in any such simply unheard-of nonsense as marrying your own stepmother."

"This confusion of her speech," Cesario thought, forlornly, "is an extremely bad symptom. She is flustered. I fear the poor fat little chucklehead is going to accept me."

Aloud, he declared, with renewed tenderness: "No, my dearest. Inasmuch as you remain technically my stepmother, I could not well compromise your fair fame by marrying you; but you could in all honor become my mistress, if only you were not so hard-hearted, and you would thus fulfil your husband's last wishes."

She regarded him, at that, with pensive if detached affection. She said:

"You really are a dear and slightly moonstricken creature, Cesario. But my husband was right, just as indeed he was almost always right, except of course about eggs."

"Yet what do you mean, Hermia—about eggs?"

"I mean he detested them; and then what in the world could you do about breakfast?"

"What, indeed?" says Cesario.

"It was most inconvenient," Hermia admitted. "Still, we had them, anyhow. And he stopped grumbling about it by-and-by. However, what I really meant was that after knowing him, I could not ever be satisfied with your glib tongue and your empty heart. There is—just as he said—no pith to you."

—Whereupon the despairing poet was silent. He smiled, then, with a restrained bitterness, a smile which was in the most noble vein of tragic heroism. He said, gloomily:

"Oh, very well! Since my happiness does not matter to you any longer—"

"Now, Cesario, I did not say that!"

"You did worse. You showed it," he rebuked her. "And besides, you keep interrupting me. What I was trying to tell you—"

"But I did not interrupt you, Cesario. I would not dream of such rudeness to anybody—"

"And what, pray, are you doing now?"

"That," Hermia replied, with large dignity, "is an entirely different matter. You had made a mistake. I thought you would like to know about it. It is not at all the same thing as interrupting anybody."

"No, to be sure," says Cesario. "You are wholly right. I apologize. What I meant to say, then, when I misguidedly thought that you had interrupted me, and when you had done nothing of the sort, was that your shrewd old rascal of a husband foresaw everything—"

"You ought to be ashamed of yourself, Cesario—" spoke the offended widow.

"Oh but, my dear, I am! I am blushing all over with contrition, I can assure you, even down to the knees. I mean only that since the omniscient dear saint regarded your being murdered with rather more concern than you do, he has ordered me to prevent your murder."

"Why, then," she returned, comfortably, "you have simply to do just what my husband told you to do, whatever it was, and everything will come out quite all right; for he understood about such matters."

—Whereupon, in the quiet convent garden, Hermia returned to her embroidery, with the calm air of one who considered the affair to have been concluded.

XLV

Now Cesario travels north; and Messire de la Forêt accompanies him, talking. To begin with, the Lord of the Forest talked about Gothic architecture, and about the average depth of the ocean (which he estimated to be 12,450 feet), and about Paracelsus' theory that all matter is composed of salt, sulphur and mercury. He spoke then about the heathen practice of head-hunting; about some superstitions as to the number seven; about the first clocks; and about the proper feeding of goldfish. He made clear the evolution of the human fœtus, and the chemical cause of the varying colors to which green leaves turn in autumn; and he touched lightly upon the gnomic poetry of the Anglo-Saxons. But he said by-and-by,—

"You begin a dangerous game."

"I cannot help that," said Cesario. "The old man has drawn me out of Branlon in order that, through a display of intrepid heroism, I might save an innocent and much persecuted woman from destruction. It is a complete nuisance; but I really do not see any open way out of the affair except for me to discomfit Hypolita's wicked plans with tact and undaunted courage."

"Indeed, my dear prince," said the Lord of the Forest, "nobody doubts that in your commerce with that rather splendid creature you will most happily combine all the superior traits of Machiavelli with the better qualities of Achilles. Yet truly it is a quaint rôle for a poet whom Branlon has applauded, to become the knight errant of his stepmother."

"It is a most ridiculous rôle," Cesario agreed—as he glanced downward, with disapproval, toward the bezoar ring on his little finger,—"especially now that my stepmother has displayed the bad taste not to be in love with me any longer."

"Oh, but come now, Cesario! you astound me."

"Nevertheless, such seems to be the case. For I have honorably proposed to make her my mistress. And she refused. Her refusal I admit to have been an immense relief, but even so, it was humiliating. In Branlon no woman ever refused me anything."

"Then why, my prince, do you not leave this unappreciative Hermia to her fate, and return with me into Branlon?"

"In fact, Lord of the Forest, I was wholly happy in Branlon until those earnest-minded Druids invaded it. Yet I am still contaminated by some traces of chivalry and even of patriotism. So I cannot well return into your bright-colored woodland kingdom until after I have preserved the kingdom of Melphé also, inasmuch as old Ferdinand has managed to take an advantage of every one of my frailties."

The Lord of the Forest shook his dark head very gravely indeed.

"If you are not careful, Cesario, these alien virtues may deliver you over to the dilapidating labors of altruism and of philanthropic endeavors; in which case, what will become of you as a poet?"

"It would mean my ruin as a poet. I know that.
And I shudder to observe that already, in some degree, I begin to lose that fortifying large contempt
for mankind in general, without which no artist
can run counter to sane public opinion, by taking
his art quite seriously. Yet at any cost I must discharge my debt of honor."

"We who are conscientious creative artists,
Cesario, cannot upon all occasions afford the luxury
of honor."

Cesario said: "That is true, of course; for one's
personal honor only too often must counsel a re-
serving where art demands a revealing. Yet I begin to fear, Lord of the Forest, that I am not indeed
a great poet."

"Eh, but do not be disheartened, Cesario; for the
deficiency is far from uncommon among all our
more widely admired creative writers."

"I do not have, I fear,"—Cesario continued, intent upon the loved labor of discussing himself—
"the emotions proper to a wholly sublime poet; or
at any rate, my emotions are not suitably intense. I
have suspected this for some while. Lately, it was
proved to me. Lately, it was my tragic lot to stand
beside the corpse of that infamous person who had

murdered both of my parents, as well as a rather large number of my other near relatives, and to find myself improperly undisturbed by his downfall. I was not choriambically inspired by the poetic justice of it. I did not—although I blush to confess my insensibility—I did not even detest the as yet combined bones and cold meat and white hair which made up his corpse."

"Alas," says the Lord of the Forest, "but with age, one detests nobody. One perceives only that men and women are sentenced malefactors, variously guilty perhaps, but all sharing unalterably the same death cell, which we call Earth. And that alone seems to matter. You cannot hate an imprisoned and condemned person who has no least chance of escape from being executed; and that such is the situation of all humankind, is a truism which in youth one ignores, and grants, actually, for the first time, with advancing age. Death is revealed to the gray-haired, with a sort of broad-minded bluntness, as the supreme and, indeed, as the sole truth—whatsoever that truth may be—for which everything that happens upon earth is but a preparing. All else is seen to be transitory, all trivial, before the vast permanence of death. So does rhetoric alone remain as the cordial of the cul-tured. For rhetoric can dull discontent as to what is bygone, by coloring all rosily; it drugs, somewhat as I am now bedrugging, the present hour; and about the future, even about death, it is the fine function of rhetoric to contrive noble fancies which beget an irrational optimism. What more could any rational person ask, than to be relieved of his rationality? But let us talk about other matters."

"Yet if we dismiss rhetoric, Lord of the Forest, how can we possibly talk about anything?"

"Well, now that all depends, my dear Cesario," replied the other, with his customary fair-minded-ness.

Why, for example (he suggested), should they not talk instructively about the fourteen Laccadive Islands, of which nine were inhabited by a people of mixed Arab and Hindu descent, called Moplas, whose main pursuit was the weaving of cocoanut fibre into buoyant cables and coarse cordage?

"Because—" said Cesario.

Or, still again, they might talk about lace, which to be sure (as the Lord of the Forest granted), was a delicate subject, inasmuch as one needed to dis-tinguish with extreme care among the drawnwork, the net, the bobbin, and the needlepoint laces. Yet furthermore, they had as a possible question of debate the surprising declaration of Philippe de Thaun, in his *Bestiary*, that God and the unicorn were the same. Now that was a theme which might be discussed almost endlessly—

"Yes," said Cesario; "but then, to the other side—"

—As was likewise (the Lord of the Forest continued) that process, now unhappily lost, through which Hellenic sculptors had managed to make ivory pliable in doing their chryselephantine work. The Egyptians, also, how had they contrived to manufacture glass which was flexible? and was it, in point of fact, the habitual custom of the older Egyptians, under the Hyksos dynasties, to stain their finger nails with henna, as so many mummies of that period suggested?

Cesario said, "Well, for my part, I think—"

But, from henna staining, the Lord of the Forest had passed on to considering the truth of various legends as to how the breast of the robin, also, procured its red staining? Then, while upon the topic of ornithology, he debated if the owl were indeed at one time a baker's daughter, as Ophelia reported?

and he so got to weighing the problem (raised by an item in the works of Pausanius) if Cecrops, the first King of Athens, might not likewise have been the first baker of bread, in the form of crescent-shaped buns, as a peace offering most acceptable to the local gods of his era?

"But now," the Lord of the Forest concluded his philosophic speculations, "we approach San Marco. And at the city-gates I must leave you, inasmuch as I could not well appear at the court of Melphé without seeming vindictive."

"I admit," returned Cesario, "that a person of your rural and taciturn habits might not—it is just possible—figure to advantage in the more talkative circles of court life. Yet what between here and Helicon can vindictiveness have to do with it?"

"My dear Cesario," replied the sublime scholar, in urbane surprise, "why, but of course I must make it my charitable fixed rule, to avoid each woman who, after having once known me, has taken up with a husband. Poor Hypolita is now married—happily enough, I believe—to your royal brother. Am I so thoughtless, or am I so completely an ingrate, do you think, that in return for my pleasant hours with her, I could allow the unfortunate creature to compare her Lorenzo with one whom, out of sheer modesty, I must leave unnamed? For me to permit any such comparison would be far worse than vindictive. It would be self-conceit. It would be out-and-out *hubris,—* than which, as I must now remind you, Cesario, there is no vice more hideous in the eyes of Heaven, or more obnoxious to the nostrils of good taste, or more remote from the nature of any philosopher."

Thus speaking, the philosopher left Cesario, at the broad drawbridge; and the last-named passed through the great gray city-gates alone, to play out, with his brother, and with his brother's wife, the game which dead Ferdinand dei Vetori had ordered.

XLVI

The five page boys who guided Cesario toward the presence of his brother were clothed handsomely, in parti-colored liveries of which the right side was russet velvet and the left side green satin; these liveries were edged with swan's down; upon the breast of each lad was embroidered, in gold thread-work, the coiled serpent of the Vetori.

They led the Prince-Cardinal, with a befitting

respectfulness, through the vast halls of the re-modeled Governor's Palace, which seemed to him too rich in gilding and, as went their ceilings, far too lavishly inhabited by impendent half-witted angels and puffy cherubs in stucco. Besides that, these halls were now cluttered up with a host of great-muscled grandiose statues, and with enormous paintings, and with bleak marble tables, and with tall funereal-looking bronze vases, and with high-shouldered cabinets filled overflowingly by bright curios. Among many mirrors and much fat furniture covered with gilded leather the boys led him likewise. Hypolita had quite changed the once shabby and gauntly furnished Governor's Palace.

In this manner did the five page boys bring Cesario into a room of which the walls displayed white doves painted on a red field, and were adorned with hunting trophies. Here the new King of Melphé received his brother with honest affection.

"You are very welcome home, Cesario," declared Lorenzo, "after your far wanderings. We drink your best health, my dear, in the noble wine of Xeres; and you must tell us all about your adventures, like a rather less pious Æneas, after supper."

Cesario said, "I fear that is not permitted me, majesty."

"No majesty, but your own brother, Cesario," returned Lorenzo, with a slight overplus of regal condescension. It was a grace which the handsome and large-hearted and wholly dear, fat creature was still practising, Cesario noted.

Then Lorenzo said, slapping his brother upon the shoulder,—

"Truly, we have heard some strange stories about your goings-on, you demure looking rascal; and your grave air causes us to believe in their truth."

"No, my brother; it is only that I have been traversing a world of minor poets. It is not the sort of place which a happily married man would understand."

Lorenzo's kindly plump face had, of a sudden, become grave and tender. He had forgotten, now, all about his monarchical "we." And in the while that Lorenzo refilled his large gold-rimmed glass, he said fondly:

"There was never any husband so happy in his wife, Cesario. My happiness troubles me. I feel that I have not deserved the love of a woman who is so beautiful and clever and virtuous."

THE TRIUMPH OF HYPOLITA

"Well, and I am free to admit, Lorenzo, that no matter how much I may admire you, I do not think you have deserved to be her husband."

"She has no fault of any kind, Cesario. She is an angel."

"And to the compassionate pure heart of an angel," says Cesario, "the situation, just now, of her unfortunate sister must be a source of considerable distress."

Lorenzo nodded, most solemnly.

"I do not exaggerate, Cesario, when I tell you that over the deplorable woman my wife has wept bucketfuls."

"Yet for my part, Lorenzo, I cannot see that in marrying the late King, and in making more happy the last hours of, so to speak, our stepfather, she did anything very disgraceful."

"That is because we men are gross-natured creatures, Cesario."

"No doubt, Lorenzo, such is the exact cause of my obtuseness."

"—For to a pure-minded woman," Lorenzo pursued, as he drank benignantly, "the mere notion of a morganatic marriage is disgusting."

"Perhaps," says Cesario.

"Moreover," Lorenzo pointed out, "we have no proof that any marriage ever took place."

"Still—" said Cesario.

"Not at all," Lorenzo returned; "inasmuch as what the woman asserts, or what King Ferdinand may have said about the matter during his dotage, does not count, of course, because both of them were directly interested parties. They may well have had left just enough sense of decency to make them lie up hill and down dale as to their marriage. We ought to believe that about them in mere charity."

"I see, Lorenzo: in mere Christian charity, we ought to believe they were lying."

"As for the sworn testimony of the priest and the five witnesses," Lorenzo explained yet further, in the while that he filled up his glass, "I have not the faintest doubt that they were all either bribed or browbeaten into their wicked and, in fact, their utterly blasphemous perjuries. It is a generally depraved state of affairs which simply shows you, Cesario, what the world is coming to, when even a clergyman acts in this way."

"It does indeed simply show me, Lorenzo."

"And besides," Lorenzo summed up, "Madonna

Hermia is quite comfortably established in her convent, with all her sewing materials at hand, in a room with a nice southern outlook. She has been given—if you ask me—a great deal more kindness than she deserves."

Thereupon Cesario smiled; and he said, with respectfulness,—

"These, beyond any question, are the bland arguments of a Christian gentlewoman."

Lorenzo grinned rather sheepishly.

"Not everyone of them would have pleased Aristotle, perhaps, as a pattern of flawless logic. But, what the devil, Cesario! you are not happily married. No happily married person, of either sex, could well expect me to squabble, with my own wife, about mere logic."

"So there is no hope, your Majesty, for Hermia's release from her prison?"

"None whatever," replied Lorenzo, affably. He then belched with extreme dignity. He poured out for himself a glass of wine; and he continued,—

"Nor is it altogether right for you, who are yourself so soon to be married, to be concerning yourself about other women."

"You give tongue to a rap on my knuckles," returned Cesario, "which reminds me I did hear, in passing, that my marriage to the Princess Christine of Lorraine had been arranged, by the late King, without anybody's having consulted me about it one way or the other."

"Why, but yes,—yes, of course," says Lorenzo. "He ought to have been more definite; for you, quite naturally, take an interest in the affair of your own marriage."

"In fact, my brother, I do admit to some selfish sense of being concerned in it."

"Well, to begin with, the Holy Father will name Marinelli to succeed you as cardinal. It is a most eligible appointment, because even apart from Marinelli's high reputation and world-famous piety, we hold safe his signed confession to three capital crimes, and so do not need to have any fear of his running counter to our interests."

"That appears to me a quite salutary arrangement, Lorenzo, in the best vein of kingcraft."

"And you are to marry Madonna Christine in June, I believe," said Lorenzo, scratching his handsome head,—"provided always that we get the Medici claim to Urbino,—and unless it seems wiser to take a princess out of Denmark, or perhaps

Sicily. However, we will let you know about all that, a little later, no doubt, in good time for the ceremony."

"I shall appreciate the courtesy, Lorenzo. Meanwhile, as you say, there is nothing like being wholly definite as to my matrimonial involvements."

Lorenzo agreed cordially; and with a benevolent gesture, he added:

"—Because no matter who your wife may turn out to be, you have only to beget a boy to reign over Melphé. It is a mere formality, Cesario. And you will probably like her well enough."

"Beyond doubt, inasmuch as Madonna Christine is so close a relative to your own first wife," Cesario returned, with point.

"Poor old dear Giovanna!" Lorenzo sighed, condoningly. "She did have her more endurable traits, after all, so near as I can remember. Yet I have not ever really regretted"—he hesitated somewhat, and then drank again—"her death. Giovanna and I, you conceive, were simply not suited to each other, Cesario. Yes; it was far better that affairs fell out as they did. For I could not make her happy here upon earth. And so it is a large comfort to me, of course, to think of her as being quite cosily settled down in

Paradise, where I daresay the angels have got more or less used to her, by this time. Her gain, in fact, was so great and so self-evident that I could not well be selfish enough to dwell upon my own deep personal loss."

Hah, and that, too (thought Cesario), sounded very much like the argument of Hypolita—an argument which did not merely justify the death of Lorenzo's first wife, but upon good moral grounds, left the slain woman in debt to her murderer. To make out of a crime an instance of rare self-sacrifice, Cesario reflected, in high admiration, was just the sort of transforming in which the new Queen of Melphé excelled.

He went then into the palace gardens, to deal with her directly. Lorenzo stayed in the room painted with white doves, where the wine was.

XLVII

"Come now, my so solemn looking brother-in-law," inquired Hypolita, when once her ladies in waiting had left them, "and is it to be peace or war between us?"

These two now stayed alone, among endless

greeneries. They sat together, upon a high-backed marble bench, among plump pillows covered with yellow satin. About them showed many alley-ways of laurel and myrtle; a half-dozen or so of woven arbors; and tall hedges of rigidly trimmed box-wood. Orange-trees scented the air. These things Cesario observed dimly, without really noticing them.

He noticed instead his own emotions. He was shaken, yet again, by the unforgotten pulsings of an adoration of which he disapproved angrily. He was very deeply flustered because these two, who had once been lovers, now met in private, for the first time since their love had left them.

Hypolita had stoutened; but to Cesario's finding, she stayed as beautiful as she had ever been; and when compared with Hypolita, no other person upon earth, as the Prince-Cardinal now compre-hended with disgust, could ever seem to Cesario of much actual importance.

He cleared his throat; and Hypolita inquired sweetly,—

"Need a staid clergyman hesitate thus long, my brother, between the bright blessings of peace and the black wickedness of warfare?"

The man answered, "Whether it be peace or war between us, majesty, is a question which it is not my privilege, but your sole right alone, to decide, now that all Melphé, and whatsoever may happen in Melphé, must depend upon your Majesty's wish."

"Indeed, that is the exact truth, Cesario," she told him, with large good-humor; "and I would prefer peace."

"Then peace let it be. Yet I must make conditions," he replied, "if but for my own self-protection."

"Do you name your terms, my brother."

"First, Hypolita," he said, with restrained but unhidden ardors, "you must not permit me to fall in love with you all over again. For I find you more beautiful than ever."

She answered, moved by an indolent frank friendliness:

"You did in truth love me—my dear brother, —somewhat greatly. And I hurt you. I am sorry."

"You caused," said Cesario, with unction, "death to touch chillingly some part of me."

"And I am sorry," Hypolita repeated. "I was sorry even then, Cesario, for you were a fine brave boy in those days. But, oh! you did bore me so insufferably, with the purity of your passion, with your respectfulness, and with your long-winded poems."

"Well, but all that, my dearest,—or at least, my former dearest,—is most happily over-past. At my age, I may no longer hope to write poems; I am not over-burdened with respect for any woman living; and my passions, nowadays, incline equably to accept the muck and sunshine of this world just as Heaven mixed them."

"In that case, Brother Cesario, we have three not unpraiseworthy traits in common; and with so much to build upon, we may fairly hope to rear a fine temple of friendship. So your first condition is granted. I give you my full permission never to fall in love with me"—Hypolita paused, and she smiled, not uncomplacently—"all over again."

"Yet, majesty, there remains a second condition."

"You have merely to name this condition, my dear brother-in-law."

"I ask, then, that Hermia shall be released from the convent of the Penitent Magdalene."

"My brother, but you exceed reason! for what have I to do with a penitent Magdalene?"

"Eh, majesty, so far as goes the penitence, nothing whatever."

A half-smiling goddess now considered him, pensively, for some while, with the most beautiful and the most innocent huge eyes which Cesario had ever seen anywhere.

"You are pleased, I believe, to become insolent."

"For the present, majesty, that contents me. Yet upon provocation, I may have to go somewhat farther in my candid speaking, before another audience."

"And whose hearing—my dear brother,—would you then poison with your absurd slanders?"

"Even the royal ears of Lorenzo, majesty, with whom I may have to deal in every sort of frankness which befits a loyal subject."

"Oh! ah!" says Hypolita. "So that is your weapon. It is double-edged, Cesario."

"Yet truth is best armed—as we both ought to remember, majesty,—when it goes naked."

Her ingenuous, fair pink-and-white face had clouded. Then she smiled affably. She said:

"In fact, you do know quite enough about our shared youth upon Gratignolles to make your base calumnies of my complete innocence unadvisable matters for Lorenzo's hearing. Yet how does the welfare of this slut concern you?"

Cesario gave every outward appearance of being horrified.

"Pardon, majesty! but you speak of a gentle-woman who—at all events, technically—is my stepmother. I cannot, therefore, permit the term 'slut' to pass unchallenged."

"If you come to that," says Hypolita, with her customary sound sense, "the snip is likewise my sister."

"Just so, majesty. And I do not think that in a convent either one of you"—here the Prince-Cardinal paused—"could live for a long while."

"No?" said Hypolita.

She stayed silent for a moment. To the left side of her tender coral-tinted lips a dimple occurred. She said, with appreciation:

"You do put things so nicely, Cesario! You have intelligence. I very often praise Heaven that Lorenzo has no intelligence in particular; but still, I can respect intelligence. For this reason, I shall be frank with you. I intend to keep every one of the fine gems which old Ferdinand left to this midget.

So it is not at all convenient that Hermia should continue to live."

"In brief, majesty, you are now bound in common-sense to commit murder so as to justify a robbery. You are wholly logical; and in view of my impending withdrawal from the Church, I have no least call to preach to you about any Divine commandments, or even about plain human decency."

"Why, but of course not, Cesario; for it is not as if I bore my sister any especial ill will. I used to be quite fond of her. However! I will show you some of the diamonds and the rubies this evening; then you can see for yourself that it would be simply foolish of me not to keep them."

"Nevertheless, majesty, I cannot permit it."

"So, my brother! and are you in love with squat Hermia nowadays?"

"Never in my life, Hypolita, have I been in love with any woman except you."

—Whereupon the Queen of Melphé appraised Cesario, now yet again, with a benign and somewhat motherly indulgence.

"I know that very well," said Hypolita. "It is that which puzzles me."

She moved closer to him, upon the garden bench,

[276]

smiling adorably; and she put her large soft arms about him, saying, with a pastoral innocence which befitted their rural surroundings:

"Kiss me, Cesario. Let us forget this stupid Hermia."

"Alas, majesty," he returned, "howsoever profoundly I may adore you, the ties of family life continue to constrain my simple and affectionate nature. So I cannot comfortably assist you either to murder my stepmother or to cuckold my brother."

Hypolita drew back, at that. Yet (as Cesario observed with relief) the tender-voiced Queen, after having gained her chief purpose, by finding out that in point of fact her brother-in-law did wear chain-armor under his doublet, now replied without anger. That she had determined to have him killed appeared certain; but it would be attended to without any ugly and ill-bred exhibition of petulance.

"I deplore your scruples," she declared, with a slightly hurt but forgiving expression. "And if I were not barren, I would tell you, in all frankness, to go to the devil. But I have no child to succeed Lorenzo. I cannot ever have a child. You, to my confusion, are his heir. Should Lorenzo die leaving me a widow—and after all, the poor self-indulgent huge infant does drink much more than is good for him—why, then you would inherit Melphé. To have you as my enemy, in that case, would be most inconvenient. So I shall have to give in to you. Do me the justice to observe that I deal with you in such frankness as is best between intelligent persons! As the price of your highly necessary good will, I agree to your second condition likewise; and that half-witted squab shall be let out of her cage."

"When?" says Cesario.

"The very moment, my brother, that I have returned from my rooms. I shall there conceal a small bit of onion in my handkerchief; and thus armed, I shall attend to our affair before supper is over. Oh, but I like you, Cesario! You are unbelievably cruel to me, Cesario: yet you appreciate women, without in the least bit understanding them; and so, it is a deep pleasure to be womanly with you as an audience. Do you observe how sad looking I am already! I am smitten with remorse, you conceive; before long, I shall be in unrestrained tears. With Lorenzo it does not pay to be subtle: the effect has to be conveyed with broad strokes. If you take cold from the dampness of my repentance, you must not blame me but only yourself, who provoked it. Let us go in, at once, to reveal the pangs of my re-awakened conscience, to Lorenzo."

She hesitated. She then kissed Cesario, vigorously, and with a sincere strange fondness.

"There!" said Hypolita; "there, Joseph! Now do you screen your blushes."

XLVIII

In the Governor's Palace a not wholly sober Lorenzo and their supper awaited them. But Hypolita retired, for an instant, because of an obligation which she modestly whispered to her husband. When she re-appeared, Hypolita did indeed have ready in her hand a handkerchief; and she displayed it to Cesario with a smile made suitably wan.

Then the King and the Queen of Melphé, with the Prince-Cardinal Cesario to the right of her Majesty, sat down to supper. Their table was not large, but it was formed throughout of pure silver, and weighed some 24,000 pounds. Hypolita inclined toward the expensive in these matters.

The seneschal raised his black gold-headed staff: and in the balcony, concealed by red silken hangings and garlands of evergreens, a choir of male sopranos, accompanied by harpsichords, theorbos and violins, began a subdued sweet music. The first course, which was served upon silver plates, was of oysters, spiced artichokes, fat carp and eels, and a jelly of the breasts of capons moulded in the form of a coiled serpent, as a tribute to the house of Vetori. Along with this course, the cellarer brought in wine, the light wine of Chablis.

Taking up his large tall glass, Cesario now observed that the bezoar stone on his little finger had become crimson; and so knew that in his hand he held death. Beyond doubt, Hypolita was a remarkably efficient creature, he reflected; a woman who acted with decision; and who attended to any requisite murder without shilly-shallying, even while fetching a handkerchief.

Cesario admired the clear lustre of his wine, and swishing it about gently, as befitted a connoisseur, he inhaled with appreciation its bouquet. He put down his glass, saying:

"A superior vintage. That is evident."

"Lorenzo," Hypolita replied, with a sob, "likes it very much with his oysters."

Lorenzo said, "But what has happened, my poor darling, that you are so sad looking?"

"It is nothing, my husband. It is only that my heart is breaking."

"Come now, my pet, but for what reason can your heart be breaking?"

"I have been talking with Cesario, my dearest," —says Hypolita, lightly touching her fine eyes with her handkerchief,—"about my unfortunate sister. And Cesario has put matters in an entirely new aspect. You have been far too harsh with my poor Hermia."

"I!" says Lorenzo; and drank wine, in discreet silence.

But Cesario, who as yet also kept silence, was observing that Hypolita, whatsoever might be her faults in the way of fornication and murder, remained conscientious as to her promises. She had not lied to him about the handkerchief. Her huge violet-colored eyes were indeed brimful of tears now that Hypolita answered Lorenzo, with benign dignity, saying:

"I would not for one moment defend her conduct, my husband, or pretend that the little bitch is worth the poot of an alley cat. It is only, just as our dear, kind great-hearted Cesario says, that it would be so much more magnanimous of you to forget and to forgive, as he puts it. Now, when you look on it in that light, and in the way a good Christian ought to look at it, Lorenzo, then it really does seem—to me, at any rate—a quite different matter."

"Perhaps you are right, my darling," Lorenzo admitted; and he drank yet more wine.

"Ah, Lorenzo, but I know I am right," she answered, as a most creditable tear welled forth from each eye. "No one of us is without sin, just as Cesario has pointed out; and so, we ought to exercise charity the one toward another. Moreover, I very much miss my poor Hermia. Oh, but I beseech of you, my husband, to pardon all her offences, no matter how disgustingly the small strumpet has conducted herself. She ought to be skinned alive! Nevertheless, let us send for her, at once, in order that I may embrace my shameless and stinking and forever dishonored but still cherished sister."

"I will do all these things," said Lorenzo, "upon condition that you, my pet, shall talk with rather more coherence, and stop crying, instantly. Upon that sole condition, let my glass be filled again; for emotion always makes me thirsty; and moreover, I like this wine; and besides that, I must drink to the poor little lady's better fortune."

"We must all three drink to her better fortune, as well as to her better behavior from now on," says Hypolita, smiling with meek gratitude at her adored master, through the bright tears of consoled anguish,—"even this staid Cesario who drinks nothing."

"I drink now," says Cesario, and you saw he was moved. "I drink to the health of the most remarkable lady in all Melphé, to her who, before my eyes, has incited the King my brother to share in that large charitableness which has always distinguished her own nature. Strangely is Melphé blessed in its Queen! For Madonna Hermia, as you both know, I desire all good: and to her better fortune I shall drink directly. Yet with due deference, it is to your health, Hypolita, my dear sister, that I must drink first."

"You honor me far too highly, my beloved brother," replied Hypolita, with a grateful and tender smile, as Cesario reached toward his death.

"However," he continued, still the prey of exalted emotions, "I must drink to you in no common tipple. Were the King's glass not in its customary state of appreciative emptiness, I would make bold to pledge you, O all-incomparable lady, from a king's own glass, right royally. As it is, I change glasses with you, sweet sister; and I drink, in that same wine which your dear lips have touched and made nectar,—To the most notable wife that was ever known in Melphé!"

He drank then.

"My dear brother," cried Lorenzo, clapping Cesario upon the shoulder, "you drink with true, thirst-inspiring eloquence; and I would indeed be a thankless dog did you drink alone."

Hypolita gasped out, "No!"

Cesario cried, "Stop, Lorenzo!"

But Lorenzo, standing, held high the tall glass which Cesario had set down before Hypolita, and in the instant that both of them tried to strike it from his hand, Lorenzo drained this glass, saying fondly,—

"To the most notable and to the best-loved wife, my own great-hearted, over-generous angel, that was ever known in Melphé!"

Hypolita stared at him. She gasped, just once. She looked then, in her desperation, at Cesario.

"You are moved, my sister?" Cesario inquired, white as paper. "I do not wonder. The devotion of the Vetori toward their wives is always a touching spectacle. Can it be there is not any antidote—for such uxoriousness?"

She replied, smiling pallidly, "I know of none."

"Nor is there any antidote needed," red-faced Lorenzo assured them. "I love my wife; her every doing is gracious in my eyes; and I do not care who tells it."

—Whereupon the King laughed tipsily. But the King's brother and the King's wife, who had once been lovers, now looked at each other, for a forlorn dreadful instant, with a mutual and an almost sympathetic intentness, because each knew that here, in the form of this boastful and slightly fuddled Lorenzo, sat a condemned man who, for every mortal purpose, was already in his dark grave.

Cesario was rather heart-stricken by this inadvertent murder in which he had played a part. He frowned, to think of how awkward, how damnably far-reaching, might be its results; but Hypolita

[285]

smiled. She smiled very sweetly, with a faint, virginal blush.

"It is not right that you two most dear and most foolish flatterers should embarrass me, in this fashion, with your eternal compliments," she declared. "So let us speak as to more important affairs than my poor virtues. I am not perfect; and none knows that more clearly than I do. Meanwhile, it would be better, I think, my husband, if you were to send a courier to-night, with an order for my sweet Hermia's instant release. Do you not think so, Cesario?"

Cesario answered her, "With your permission, my sister, I myself shall become that courier—to-morrow."

Now the King's wife looked at the King's heir levelly; and she said, levelly:

"To-morrow let it be. To-morrow, Cesario, all matters hereabouts shall be at your disposal."

Then the cellarer brought round the red wine of Cyprus spiced with pistachios and cinnamon and cloves. A trumpet sounded to announce the coming of the roast boar's head and the roast peacocks. These dainties were served upon golden plates, along with a large pasty of mushrooms.

XLIX

To this dish of mushrooms, of which his Majesty had partaken perhaps over freely at supper, the King's physicians, in the most resonant sort of Latin, attributed the King's sudden illness; and after purging him, they induced his body's comfort with opiates.

"You will be up again within two days, my dearest," Hypolita assured him, with a somewhat haggard but resolute smiling.

—To which Lorenzo replied only: "Send for Prince Cesario. And then let everyone else withdraw."

"I am here, my brother," said Cesario, at the bedside.

"O Brother Cesario," said Lorenzo, turning restively among the heaped white pillows, "O Brother Cain! need I tell you I am poisoned?"

"Such is not the opinion of your physicians, Lorenzo."

"At this hour, my brother, I, who am perhaps not noted for my wisdom, am more wise than they are. I know I am dying, no matter what they may tell me. I know that you have poisoned me, because no other person gains by my death. You should not dispute these plain syllogisms, Cesario."

"It is true, Lorenzo, that through your death I would gain Melphé. But I abhor Melphé. I most certainly do not desire Melphé."

"So I had thought, Cesario, for you are gaining only a new title and a great deal of trouble. The budget of Melphé alone is enough to wreck any merely human mind. Yet if it was not you, then who has poisoned me?"

"Chance, Lorenzo, blind chance. Oh, and blind love!"

"Your voice shakes, Cesario. You know the truth. Do you now tell me the truth, my brother, for I am dying, and I would die at peace with you, because you were once my very little chubby brother at Arvieto, before we became royal persons."

Cesario obeyed him. Speaking unreservedly, in this hushed, drug-scented room—where the firelight pulsed intermittently through the steady glow of three ivory lamps,—Cesario told Lorenzo how the King of Melphé had drunk death in pledging the Queen of Melphé. And the King, listening, propped up among many pillows, began to smile.

"She has always loved jewels," he said, gently, with a slight air of apology, "and Madonna Hermia had the most handsome jewels in Melphé. Yes: I can quite understand that Hypolita would have killed both of you in order to keep these jewels. That was not right of her, I admit; and I am sorry she should have upset your visit to us in this inconsiderate fashion."

"Ah, but, my dear," Cesario protested, "in the bosom of one's family, nobody expects to find the milk of human kindness."

"Even so, you must not punish her, Cesario, when you are King. You must promise me that."

"I regret to refuse you. But I cannot pardon her, Lorenzo! for it is through her vanity and through her greed and through her ruthlessness, my so foolish, great-hearted brother, that you are now entering into Paradise."

"You are optimistic," said Lorenzo, dryly; and he then continued, lying back among many heaped-up pillows, with his dark hair much tousled, and with his plump handsome face now strangely gaunt looking:

"No; she is not perfect; but I have loved her. You poets write about love so incessantly that you have not any time left in which to understand it. Do you let the fact suffice that I take my death contentedly enough from her to whom I owe the great joy of my life. Indeed, Cesario, the discomforts of this moment appear trivial when I weigh them against the happiness which I have shared with Hypolita. I may now tell you—since the candor of a dying man costs him nothing—that in order to marry her, I killed my first wife in cold blood; but I have never regretted it. And I must be punished presently, it may be, for having killed poor lean, shrill Giovanna; yet not even in hell, my brother, shall I regret the price with which I bought the love of Hypolita. The saints have their joy in heaven, so we are told. I do not grudge these saints their eternal psalm-singing. I have had my joy upon earth. Hypolita has made my life all wonderful for me; and my fond love of Hypolita no flaming fiend shall ever dig out of my heart with his pitchfork."

Cesario said, "You blaspheme; you speak foollishly: and I envy you."

"You may well envy me, you poor lean piddling fidgeting phrase-making Cesario! for my sins have been large pleasant sins, and they end happily now, without any ugly shadow of repentance. Were it all

[290]

to do again, I would do it all, king or no king. King Ferdinand was a great monarch: I was not. Yet I have lived handsomely, in open sunlight, as befitted a man; at nights I have taken my pleasure in the bed of Hypolita: while he fared shrewdly, like an old dusty spider, eternally weaving in some corner or another. To-morrow we shall both be silent stinking dirt. But I would not change lives with the empire-builder, Cesario, not even for the fine bribe of his so much finer epitaph. Well! and so I give up to you my crown; but in return, you must give me your promise to permit Hypolita to leave Melphé unhurt and in all honor."

"I promise it, then, my dear," said Cesario, "even though, as I must tell you frankly, your wife's conduct in killing you has caused her to forfeit my esteem."

"In that event, all is most happily settled,— your Majesty," returned Lorenzo, smiling. "Now then, let us have in my confessor, because even though I die unrepentant, yet a king owes it to his people to set them a pious example—'when once he is old enough to make all his doings appear venerable.' Dear me, but how long ago it was, and in what very different circumstances, I proclaimed that truth to Hypolita!" the dying man remarked, with a small chuckle. Then Lorenzo said cheerily:

"Well, I am old enough now. I have had a glad time upon earth. I regret nothing. Yet let us have in my confessor; and I will lie to the poor good shorn simpleton, with as much pious civility as I can manage, because to commit that sacrilege is my last duty now as a king."

L

Coming from the last drugged, painless, and just half-heartedly fretful death-throes of Lorenzo, into the Queen's apartments, upon the north-east side of the Governor's Palace, Cesario found all quiet within. But outside, a new day was dawning; birds chirped, and they twittered disputatiously, outside. At each one of the six windows, between the drawn curtains, showed a pallid, perpendicular, thin sliver of daylight. He had not entered this room, as Cesario now recollected, since the evening of Duke Sigismund's funeral, when dead Gratiano and dead Sebastian and dead Lorenzo had talked together here, with a Cesario who was now equally dead.

At that remote season, this room had not smelled so strongly of dried roses and lavender. Cesario parted the oppressive window-curtains, pair by pair. He found time to dislike the fuzzy feel of their heavy velvet. Then, turning about, he saw that before him—just where Sebastian had half-drawn his dagger against Gratiano—stood Messire de la Forêt. Between Cesario and the sublime scholar —lying upon a small low couch, precisely as once had lain the body of Cesario's mother—lay now the second Queen of Melphé.

She remained motionless. Her fine body appeared, indescribably, flattened. She was exceedingly beautiful in the shadowless, mild light of dawn. When compared with Hypolita, nobody else could ever seem of much actual importance.

Her right hand as yet held the vial of poison with which she had killed herself, Cesario observed meditatively. And he observed also, with a continuing reflective interest, that which he had never noticed before: Hypolita very much resembled his mother. Hypolita, as he now knew with a vague sense of wonder, had always reminded both Cesario and Lorenzo of their mother, without either of them having ever perceived this fact before to-day, this new day, this most bothersome day.

"Yet the sun rises just as calmly," he reflected, "and the birds argue over their breakfast quite as lightheartedly, as if a Cesario were not involved in this solemn pickle. One could well make a poem out of the vast unconcern of the universe with our human fretfulness, even when a Cesario is being rather seriously annoyed. And Hypolita is dead! By-and-by I shall comprehend that fact. My emotions, as yet, are not rising suitably to the occasion."

And he thought also: "For I am wishing—of all preposterous notions!—that my mother were here. She understood me. She protected me, always. She would understand that I am only her frightened baby Cesario, with unduly prolonged legs, disguised as a king. And she is not anywhere. Gray worms have quite eaten up the soothing large warm breasts against which she used to cuddle me, half contemptuously, but so very lovingly. I shall not ever again touch that dear, genial, gross-minded handsome strumpet, who comprehended and petted me. I am alone. I shall always be quite alone until this pumping muscle, here under my hand, stops pumping, and so rids me of a child's ever-present timidity as to a world I cannot understand."

Afterward he spoke, with a tranquil and king-like dignity.

"So, Lord of the Forest," said Cesario, "this infamous woman was afraid of my justice now that I ascend the throne of my fathers. And it was to no effect that I promised my poor murdered brother his destroyer should come to no harm."

"I cannot wholly agree with your Majesty," replied the Lord of the Forest—who as yet stood upon the other side of the couch, looking down toward the dead Queen, in reflective consideration. "Madonna Hypolita regarded your deceased brother with a sincere affection; through a seeming contradiction such as is not infrequent in married life, she deluded him but yet loved him: above all, she did not wish to survive him in the fallen estate of a deposed and exiled queen. But you, your Majesty! ah, no, she did not ever fear you, Cesario, not for one instant, because she believed that you loved her."

"Yet need I tell you with what an utter loathing I detested this wicked creature, this sleek murderess?"

[295]

The Lord of the Forest shrugged.

"Why, but yes, that is true enough. Still, you loved her not any whit the less; and she knew it."

To that statement Cesario answered with a certain uncertainty.

"In fact, Lord of the Forest, I do not know whether I more loved or more hated this woman who lies dead here, and who is no longer a lovely peril to mankind. She was wholly agreeable to look at; she was great-spirited; she had the fine intelligence of a serpent. Yet she resembled all humankind, in that she made some slips from strict virtue; and she was guilty of her noticeable errors in judgment—as when, to cite but a single instance, she attempted to murder me, and when I was a large deal too clever for her."

"Most handsomely has your great cleverness been rewarded, Cesario, now that your saga ends in the approved fashion of an ancient fairy tale. You are about to marry a young princess, and to become a king; and one can but envy your all-glorious fortune."

"Indeed," said Cesario, gloomily, "I cannot betray old Ferdinand's faith in me. I am truly his last living heir—the heir, not of his body, but of his purpose, that purpose which I respect rather than cherish. So I must stay here, in this world which he made. I cannot ever return to Branlon. Instead, I must see to it that his people keep their contentment and their small dull pleasures. I must be king over Melphé; and I must serve, according to the best of my ability, that stolid and stupid and sane Melphé which the old thieving murderer created to be a benefit to the stolid and stupid and sane run of mankind."

"Eh, Cesario"—and up went the eyebrows of the sublime scholar,—"since when did you begin to love the run of mankind?"

"Never at any instant, Lord of the Forest. But if I do not take the throne"—here Cesario smiled— "why, then the town band will not continue to play in the plaza."

"Yet need that matter very much to you, Cesario, when you might be going about Branlon making a more noble music?"

"Yes, Lord of the Forest; for all would be as if Ferdinand dei Vetori had never lived; and his stolid, stupid, sane work would perish. I cannot permit that. He would not like it," Cesario declared, as if this circumstance quite explained matters. "So his work must go on; and gray, grave mediocrity must keep its triumph."

It was a sentiment which the Lord of the Forest applauded, with his not-ever-failing and urbane and obscurely amused benevolence.

"Come now," says he, "but this is indeed most gratifying. For you have ascended, after all, Cesario, into the praiseworthy ways of altruism; and your inner nature has become purified and ennobled just as remarkably as your worldly fortune has prospered."

"I cannot well help that, Lord of the Forest. I have tried my utmost to follow after the bright and more excellent fashion of Branlon. But the old man was too strong for me; he was too shrewd; and so, at last, he has bound me over to serve his irrational and, indeed, his immoral desire to help human beings some little way toward orderly and contented living."

A pause followed. You could hear the birds outside, in exceedingly high spirits over the dawn of this new day which had conferred upon Melphé a new monarch.

"I look into the future," declared the grave Lord of Branlon—nodding wisely his proud dark head in the as yet dusky room,—"and I foresee that throughout the remainder of your life you, whom the old man has conquered, will reign over Melphé in a continuing prosperity."

"Hah!" says Cesario, groaning.

"Yours will prove to be a reformation far more noteworthy than was that of Lysander, my time-ruined poet: for you will extirpate that corruption which has invaded the courts of justice; you will assist commerce by many prudent fiscal reforms; you will give over your entire attention to state affairs and to well-considered measures for the welfare of the kingdom at large."

"And yet all this long dreary while," said Cesario, "I shall be detesting that kingdom! and in secret I shall always hunger for the green aisles of Branlon, that forest without any fault, that wood without withering."

"You will get on tolerably, Cesario, with the young Princess of Lorraine. You will increase the navy. You will balance the budget. You will maintain a sound foreign policy. You will prosper, among your subjects' not-ever-failing applause, at every moment of your life, as a monarch but a little less competent than was King Ferdinand."

[299]

Cesario replied only, with a stoic's glum heroism:

"Still, I might have fared worse. To marry a beautiful young princess, and to become a king, and to reign gloriously forever afterward, is not the most luckless of human fates."

"It is, as I can but repeat, the conventional climax of every well-builded fairy tale," agreed the Lord of the Forest, shrugging yet again. "And so your saga ends happily."

"I think otherwise," returned Cesario; "but for the ageing poet there is not any help against the tyranny of time and common-sense. Under that tyranny, Cesario becomes Ferdinand; such is the story of each human generation; and one does not find in it any varying. I am doomed henceforward to live as a useful member of human society: there is no hope for me! So let us now part here, beside the corpse of my dead love, of my dead youth. Let us part amicably, as befits a pair of friendly monarchs; and let each of us get back to the affairs of his decreed kingdom."

With that decided upon, the Lord of the Forest departed jauntily into Branlon, where young dreams honored him forever. But Cesario returned to his courtiers and his captains and his lackeys, to be crowned as King in the Cathedral of San Marco, and to enter into that famousness which now enshrines his name; and which keeps his memory immortal in the proud annals of Melphé.

www.ingramcontent.com/pod-product-compliance
Lightning Source LLC
Chambersburg PA
CBHW031200020726
47499CB00002B/433